Rafe and the Redhead

GERRY BARTLETT

DEDICATION

To my loyal fans who wanted Rafe's story, especially the
Facebook Real Vampires Fan Group who picked our
Rafe's picture. He's just what I imagined! Sigh.

CHAPTER ONE

God, but he hated weddings. And this one had all the trappings of a mortal's dream come true. Hilarious since there were less than a handful of mortals scattered among the two hundred guests here tonight. He'd never thought his best friend would have gone for this kind of thing. Long white dress, bridesmaids.

Rafe made quick work of the fine Scot's whiskey that the groom had demanded be served along with champagne. Then Glory threw the bouquet into a crowd of squealing single women. It figured. His very pregnant lady caught it. Lacy turned toward him, her face glowing with happiness. Oh, yeah. She wanted to be next. Desperately. Shit.

"You're up, Valdez." A hand clamped on his shoulder.

Rafe caught himself before he growled and threw a punch. Of course the wedding singer would be right behind him, ready to push him into the crowd of single guys for the garter toss.

"Touch me again, Caine, and I'll take your arm off." Okay, so he did have a growl in him. Israel Caine laughed, stupid ass.

"No you won't. You can't ruin our gal's wedding. So

1

we'll both get up there and try to not catch the fucking garter." Caine elbowed Rafe, apparently not caring that he was tempting fate. "Look at Blade, sliding that garter down Glory's leg. Oh no he didn't. Copped a feel in front of God and everybody." He covered his eyes and moaned in exaggerated pain. "Can you believe it?"

"Fool." Rafe planted his own elbow to do maximum damage then strode toward Lacy when he saw her wince and rub her stomach. "Baby, you all right?"

"Just the babies doing gymnastics. I'm fine. But did you see? Glory aimed this right at me." She smiled and leaned in to smell the bouquet. White roses and a bunch of other flowers Rafe couldn't name.

"I saw you leaping for it." Rafe grinned. "If you'd landed on your stomach, how would that have looked?"

"A cat always lands on her feet, lover." Lacy reached out and ran her finger down his cheek. "You going to try for the garter or not?"

"Sure he is." Caine was there again. "He can't wait. Right, Valdez?" He nodded and the drummer on the bandstand hit the cymbals.

"Gentlemen here who are still single," Richard Mainwaring, best man for the groom, stood at the microphone. "Come up here. Blade is ready to throw the garter. I know you all want to be next to marry." He winked at his bride who was one of the bridesmaids. "Misery loves company, so we're not letting any of you hang back." He ducked when a high heel whizzed past his head. "Kidding, darling. Of course I highly recommend wedded bliss."

Rafe snorted then realized Lacy was giving him a narrow look. "Okay, I'm going. Stay back from this, Lace, it might turn into a brawl. Because, much as we love our ladies, you know marriage isn't exactly on any guy's top ten list."

"You do the crime, you should do the time." Caine shoved Rafe forward. "Don't worry, Lacy. I'll put him front and center."

"Didn't I warn you about touching me?" Rafe wheeled on the man. "You must not care if you lose your fangs and have to drink blood from a straw."

"Don't go up there on my account." Lacy backed up, heading for the safety of the buffet table. "Thanks, Ray, but I know my guy isn't ready to marry me. He's still carrying a torch for you know who."

"Fuck. See what you've done?" Rafe shoved Caine away from him.

"I didn't do a damned thing. She's not wearing your ring, is she?" Ray nodded toward Lacy who was surrounded by women checking out her bouquet. "It was me? I'd want to stake my claim. Heard it was triplets. The woman needs security, backup. What promise does she have you won't disappear some night?"

"Like you're a fucking expert on relationships." Rafe seriously wanted to plant a fist in the vampire's smug face. "I don't owe you an explanation but I've got a ring in my pocket." He turned toward the stage. Yeah, he had one. Had been carrying it for three weeks. Just couldn't pull the trigger. Blade, the groom, was twirling the lacy blue garter over his head and looking over the crowd of men who, as one, seemed to have decided to check their pockets.

"Listen to me, all of you. If this thing hits the ground next to any man, I'm personally pounding that individual into a bloody pulp. You hear me, lads?" Blade let his brogue show as he glared at the reluctant crowd He'd imported a dozen relatives from his native Scotland and at least four of them were stuck in the single guy melee. "Now hands up. Courage. I can't make you marry, ye ken. It's a game, that's all. Ready?" And he tossed the thing, straight at Rafe.

Instinct took over, a thousand years of it. Rafe snatched it out of the air before he could stop himself. Caine clapped him on the back. The other men sighed in relief then roared with laughter, probably at his look of pain.

Rafe glanced toward the buffet table and saw Lacy's eyes fill with tears. What the hell? Did that mean she was happy that fate was pushing them toward the altar? Or something else? He was damned if he could read her moods as her pregnancy progressed. He slid the garter up the sleeve of his suit and stopped next to the happy couple for a quick picture. Of course there was a wedding photographer. Just one more freaking tradition. Lightning streaked the sky and thunder boomed even though it was a clear night. Glory's parents, excited and a little upset by the whole vampire thing, kept it lively with their Olympus magic. Score one for the nontraditional side.

"Anyone seen Lacy?" Rafe couldn't find her once the photo ops were over.

"She went toward the fence. Wanted some air, she said." One of the other clerks from the shop where Lacy was manager helped herself to wedding cake. "She left the bouquet on the table. So I know she'll be back."

Rafe strode toward the fence that bordered their vampire host's lavish estate. It was on a hilltop with a view of the city of Austin. Other couples had strolled over to enjoy the view and there were benches where you could sit if you wanted to stay a while. He finally spotted Lacy on one under a tree.

"Hey. I was looking for you. Are you feeling okay?" He sat next to her and picked up her hand. It was a chilly December night, the winter solstice, so this party could go on for hours yet. But her hand was warm. Shape-shifters, even were-cats like Lacy, ran hot.

"Physically, I'm fine." She sighed and kept gazing at the lights of the state capitol building in the distance.

"What's that supposed to mean? Talk to me. I'd think you'd be happy. It was a nice wedding, your boss is finally hitched to her soulmate and you caught the bouquet. What's wrong with that?" He started to turn her face toward his but remembered she hated for him to do that. Women. Mysterious creatures. And when they were a cat too? Impossible to understand. Which was part of the excitement too.

"Are you upset? That Glory is married now?" She finally looked at him. "I know you love her."

"Aw shit. Are we going over that again?" Rafe dropped her hand. This was an old issue and getting older. "I love her like a friend now. Once it was more. You know we hooked up. But she loves Blade. Enough to marry him. I'm not so stupid that I'm going to pine after a woman who loves another man. I've moved on. To a woman I know loves me back. Who sees me as someone who can be number one in her life. I *am* your number one, right?"

"Yeah. But maybe that makes *me* stupid." Her eyes glittered and she looked back at the city lights.

"No, it makes you wonderful. I love you, Lace." He put his hand over her burgeoning stomach. "I love that you're carrying my babies." He squatted down in front of her and tugged on her hands. "Look at me. I've been holding onto this for a couple of weeks, waiting for the right time."

She looked down at him. "What?"

He dug in his coat pocket. "This. Will you marry me?" He popped open the ring box and showed her he'd gone all out. He'd asked her sister to help him and the ring was vintage, which Lacy loved, and set in platinum. The diamond was a good size and the ring should fit.

She stared at him then stared at it. The silence stretched until Rafe was beginning to wonder if she was sick or something.

"Your timing sucks."

"Why? I was going to do this the other night but you came home with a headache. Then I had that emergency at the club and had to stay late. You were asleep when I got home."

"Excuses." She snarled. Yeah, just about to let her cat out. He knew the signs. "You waited until Glory tied the knot. Is married to Blade and off the market. Then, then you can commit to me." She jumped up, knocking him on his ass in the grass. "Sorry, Rafe, but I won't take Glory's leftovers."

"Wait." Rafe jumped up and took off after her. She did go cat on him then and leaped over the fence. Shit on a stick. It was dangerous for her in her condition to take off over that pointed iron and he knew the thing was electrified. Luckily she cleared it by a foot. His woman. She was powerful and beautiful in her red-gold fur. After he tucked that ring back in his pocket, he shifted himself, choosing a large bird that soared overhead. He kept track of her, aggravated that instead of heading to the home they shared on Sixth Street, she was going toward her family's compound further south.

She followed the lake front until she hit the wooded acreage that surrounded the cluster of homes where the were-cats lived. Then she shifted again. He saw her look down to make sure she was still presentable, brushing her hair back behind her shoulders, before she strolled toward the porch lights of her mother's mansion.

Rafe landed behind her, shifting again so they could talk. "Stop! Lacy, please don't go in there."

"Why not? I'm always welcome even if I was stupid enough to get knocked up by a common shifter." She sniffed, flinging her hair like a flame-colored banner. "I guess I'm just one of those women who never learn. Always picking emotionally unavailable men."

"That's not fair. I'm available. I laid my heart at your feet not five minutes ago." Rafe stepped in front of her and put his hands on her shoulders. God, she was beautiful—tall and graceful even when swollen with pregnancy. She had slim legs under her short skirt and creamy shoulders that were set off by the emerald green dress she'd chosen for the wedding. The shawl she'd thrown over the skimpy dress must have been left on the bench when she'd shifted. She shivered and he tried to put his arms around her. She shook her head.

"Stop it. I didn't see your heart at my feet. What I saw

was a willingness to commit. Good for you. Am I supposed to pin a medal on you? You *are* willing to step up." She must have read something in his face. "Oh, yes, I heard that's what you said. That you were stepping up." She looked away, her eyes glittering. "I won't be your pity partner, Rafe. If you'd offered me a ring even a month ago, when Glory was still missing, I would have taken it gladly. But now?" She shoved him out of the way. "I'll have to think about it."

"Those babies are mine, Lacy. No matter what you need to think about, know this. I am their father and I will be in their lives from the minute they are born." He followed her all the way to her mother's door. No surprise when the door flew open before Lacy could reach for the doorknob.

"Get out of here, shifter. My daughter has come home where she belongs." Mama Cat showed her claws. "She will let you know if she wishes to see you again."

"Mama, stay out of this." Lacy turned and faced him one more time. "Of course you can see the babies. But I know your kind. If these children are were-cats, you won't care to raise them. They will repulse you. Can you deny that?"

"Damn right I deny that." Rafe didn't bother to respond when Mama Cat hissed. "They are my blood. Which means something in my world. You will not keep me from them. Cat or not, they will know their father. Learn from me. And, Lacy, I meant what I said." He reached for her again, refusing to let go when she tried to squirm away from him.

"Blame it on hormones or something but all of this resistance is crap. I know you love me and I love you. Marry me and let's raise these children together. Make a home together. Stop this foolishness and accept my ring. You want a big wedding like Glory just had? We can do that. Whatever you want." He pulled her close and kissed her, putting everything he had into it. He could feel Mama

Cat about to pounce but knew she wouldn't hurt her daughter. When Lacy's mouth opened under his, he knew he was winning.

"Rafael, son of Emiliano, grandson of Matias, you must come with us." The voice boomed out of the darkness.

Rafe jerked back from Lacy and turned to put her behind him. He knew that voice even though he hadn't heard it in a hundred years or more. He looked around and saw at least two dozen pairs of gleaming eyes in the darkness. The cats. They'd heard what they'd consider a threat and clearly were ready to rumble. Not to help him but to protect Lacy and her mother.

"Tomas. What do you want?" He had come away without a weapon. Shit. Damian, who owned the estate where the wedding had been held, had made them all surrender their weapons at the door when they'd arrived. It had been a wise precaution considering the variety of paranormals attending. Rafe could shift now, get away, but he knew Tomas and his backup would just shift after him.

"Your grandfather commands your presence. Come with us." Tomas stepped into the pool of light from the porch. Of course he looked the same. Immortals didn't age after thirty or so. He was still dark, dangerous and cocky. A real bastard tonight, though they'd been close once.

"You know I don't serve my grandfather now. We came to an understanding more than a century ago." Rafe nodded as the cats moved closer but held up one hand. Tomas toyed with a pistol that looked like the handheld version of a machine gun, the kind that could shoot many rounds, fast. Rafe wasn't about to let the cat family be slaughtered.

"Things have changed. Grandfather is dying. He calls you to his side. We have no time to waste. Will you come on your own or do we make this happen the hard way?" Tomas smiled like he hoped Rafe chose to make it hard on all of them. He glanced around the clearing. "Collateral damage might be necessary." There were hisses from the darkness. The cats were saying "Bring it on."

"How can an immortal be dying?" Lacy decided to get involved.

"I don't answer to a cat." Tomas spat on the ground.

The answering hiss from a dozen cats made the hair on the back of Rafe's neck rise. Had he heard a rifle cock? That was all he needed, a shootout with no one the winner.

"Manners, Tomas. This is my fiancé, Lacy Devereau. You are on her parents' property and should show respect. If you can't manage that, then leave."

"Not without you, brother."

Rafe heard Lacy gasp. Yeah, she hadn't a clue about his family. For good reason. "All right. I'll come. But Lacy asked a valid question. How is it that my immortal grandfather is dying?" He said it calmly but part of him, a part deep inside where he'd buried it long ago, stirred and moaned. Grandfather, who'd made him into the man he was today, dying? Not possible.

"He was poisoned. It's a new weapon developed by an old enemy. We've tried everything but can find no antidote. So he's been wasting away. Time is short now, Rafael. Come." Tomas sneered at Lacy. "Marrying a cat? That should finish the old man if nothing else does." He turned on his heel and half-dozen men, who had blended into the trees, emerged to surround him.

"Rafe!" Lacy ran to his side and threw her arms around him. "Be careful."

"I will." He kissed her one more time. The babies kicked him in the stomach and he grinned. "My children just told me good-bye. I have a lot to live for. Of course I'll hurry back. Start planning our wedding."

"Or your funeral." Mama Cat had to have the last word.

Rafe ignored her and strode after his brother. A huge SUV that had been left on the road leading into the estate roared to life as the men piled inside.

"We aren't shifting there?" He'd been given the front passenger seat and his brother was driving. The other men were crowded into the two back seats.

"You know how far it is. This isn't the dark ages, brother. We have a private jet waiting for us. The old man has plenty of money so we go in style." Tomas glanced at him, taking in the custom tailored suit he'd worn to the wedding. "You seem to be doing well except for your choice in women."

"Don't start, Tomas. I'll plant my fist in your face if say one more word about my fiancé." Rafe held on when Tom took a corner too fast. That was his brother, always reckless. "As I recall, you never stuck with one woman long enough to make a commitment." That got a laugh from the men in the back. "What?" He looked back and recognized one of his cousins.

"Just wait, Rafael. After you left, your grandfather arranged a marriage for Tomas. To Lucia Escalante. Tomas is whipped, I tell you. He has seven children and we lost count of how many grandchildren." His cousin nudged the man next to him. "Lucia makes sure Tomas is true to her or there would be hell to pay, eh, cousin?"

"Shut up, Nico." Tomas jerked the car to a stop at a red light. "Lucia is plenty of woman for any man." He glanced at Rafe. "And she gave me fine children. I saw that cat is carrying. Yours?"

"Yes." Rafe gave his brother a hard look. "I know what you're thinking. Whatever they are, I will accept and raise them."

"Grandfather will never have another half breed in the camp. You were bad enough but at least your mama was a higher level demon so you brought something special to the table. But a were-cat?" Tomas glanced back at his men and let out a cat-like howl. "*Pobrecito.* Grandfather will never let you keep her."

Lacy paced the floor. "I can't believe they just dragged

him out of here." She turned when the front door flew open, sagging when it was just her sister, Amy.

"Well, you don't have to look so disappointed. Are you wearing it? The ring?" She snatched Lacy's hand. "What the hell? Has Rafe proposed yet or not?"

"He made it clear he wants to marry you." Lacy's mother jumped up from her seat on the couch in front of the fireplace. "I'm pleased you obviously turned him down." She grabbed Lacy and kissed her cheek. "A marriage would be unthinkable. You will have the babies of course. We will be happy to raise them here in the safety of the family. But then you must take a suitable mate. Leo--"

"You can't possibly think to start that again. Not now." Lacy threw off her mother's hands. "I love Rafe. We fight. So what? All lovers fight. At least around here." She sank down in an upholstered chair and, to her horror, burst into tears.

"Lacy!" Her sister sat on the chair's padded arm next to her. "What happened? Did he propose?"

"Yes." Lacy took the tissue from the box her mother threw into her lap. It was all the sympathy she'd get from Mama and she knew it. "After Glory was safely married to Blade. I told Rafe to shove it."

"No!" Amy punched her on the arm and got up to sit beside her mother on the couch. "How stupid can you be? He loves you. We went ring shopping together. He wanted you to have the perfect ring. It's vintage just like you wanted and the diamond! Enormous. Did you at least get to see it?"

"Yes." Fresh tears. Of course she'd seen it. It *had* been perfect. Exactly what she would have picked for herself. Did that mean he really did love her? Would have married her even if Glory St. Clair had suddenly dumped Blade and come running to Rafe for a hot reunion? Lacy buried her face in a wad of tissues. Who was she kidding? Glory had powers, first dibs, a lot of things *she* would never have.

And years of history with Rafe.

"Stop it." Amy was next to her again, her hand on Lacy's shoulder. "I bet you're comparing yourself to Glory. Have you looked in a mirror lately? You're beautiful, smart and any guy would be lucky to have you."

"I'm carrying forty pounds of kittens in my lap, which has disappeared completely. I can't see my feet and I'll probably have stretch marks. As a bonus my hair is falling out." Lacy heard her mother sigh. "What?"

"I gave you that cream to rub on your stomach. You should use it." Her mother got up and pulled Lacy to her feet. "You need to go to bed. Give yourself a chance to rest. That man is gone now and his absence will give you time to see things clearly, without all of your cat-passions clouding your mind." She smiled. "Oh yes, I know your blood runs hot, my sweet girl. But be wise. Don't tie yourself to him just because you let your hormones rule your heart."

"Mama…" Lacy knew her face was flaming. She was in no mood for this lecture which she'd heard too many times now. Of course she was passionate. So was Rafe. They set the sheets on fire when they were together. Just thinking about being with him made her thighs clench.

"Oh, I can't stand to look at you. Go ahead. Pine away for your lover." Her mother stepped back when she noticed Lacy's claws were showing. "But, trust me, tomorrow everything will look better. And the longer Rafael is away, the easier it will be for you to see that he is wrong for you." She held up her hand, her own claws showing now. "One last thing. I don't mind Glory, even if she is a vampire, since I believe she's been fair to you. But if her relationship with Rafael worries you, quit the job in her shop and cut ties."

"No, I like my job. I'm the manager and she's leaving tonight for her honeymoon. She counts on me to keep the shop running smoothly while she's gone. I'm even cat-sitting for her. Boogie is at my house, *our* house, right now." Fresh tears. That had to stop. "I'm going home. Where I live with Rafe. I do love him and I'm going to marry him as soon as he gets back." Lacy kissed her mother's cheek. Of course Mama was frowning now. "I want to know how his brother found him here. Someone tracked him and I think I know who did."

"Uh oh. I see that look. Are you on the warpath now?" Amy grinned. "Okay, I know, not funny. But surely Rafe's family won't hurt him. If his grandfather is dying, Rafe may want to say good-bye. Has he told you about his past? His life in the clan?"

"No. He left there long ago. They had a falling out. That's why they had to drag him back, I guess. So I don't like the fact that someone we trusted was obviously sent to Austin from wherever the hell his home is to spy on him." Lacy stepped closer to the fireplace. "Can you drive me to my apartment, Amy? I'm worn out from shifting and cold."

"You should have dressed more sensibly tonight in something a little warmer, darling." Her mother picked up a throw and draped it around her shoulders.

"I wanted to look good for this wedding." Lacy sighed. Foolish of her. Glory had been radiant and Rafe had watched her walk down the aisle with love in his eyes. He insisted it was a friend's love. She had to believe him or turn into a jealous shrew.

"You look beautiful even if more appropriate for a June wedding instead of a winter one. And I'm sure you outshone the bride even with forty pounds of precious babies in your stomach." Her mother smiled, as usual reading her motives accurately. "Go. Take care of your boss's cat and sleep. We'll talk more later." She nodded at Amy. "Drive her home."

"Sure. Maybe I'll spend the night. That okay with you, sis?" Amy picked up car keys from a table by the door.

"Yes, I'd like the company." Lacy shivered again. Where was Rafe now? How were they getting there and what was his family like? How far away was this mysterious shifter territory? They hadn't talked about his past and she hadn't pushed. Which she now realized was a mistake. But she suspected she knew exactly who could and would give her answers. First thing tomorrow she was getting some. Or that spy was going to regret ever coming to Austin and worming into their lives.

CHAPTER TWO

"What the hell has happened here?" Rafe had had the long plane ride to think about his home. He'd pictured the neat village with his grandfather's large lodge near the center. Dozens of houses surrounded the stone three-story building that was not only his grandfather's home, but the meeting place for the shifter clan. Now, looking around, Rafe barely recognized it.

"Grandfather has been ill a long time. And you sure weren't around to see to things." Tomas wouldn't look at him. He put the van in park and turned off the engine.

"What were *you* doing?" Rafe stepped out and looked around. There was trash in the courtyard. One of the houses had obviously burned down and the charred remains hadn't been cleared away. This would never have been tolerated before he'd left. Roofs had missing shingles, paint was peeling and more than one had sagging shutters. He felt like he'd stumbled upon a village that was suffering from hard times, not the prosperous place he'd expected.

"I was busy." Obviously glad for the distraction, Tom laughed when a beautiful woman ran into him, wrapping her arms around him.

"You took long enough. Where was this brother of

15

yours, Antarctica?" She pulled Tom's face down for a kiss, then twisted his ear. "Or did you spend some time enjoying yourself before you looked for him?"

"Lucia, this is Rafael." Tom dragged her around the car to meet him. "He was in Texas, if you can believe it. Right where we were told he would be. Have you looked at a map? It took a while to get there and back. Then we had to track him down."

Rafe nodded to Tom's wife. "A pleasure to meet you, Lucia. We've been on the plane for hours. It's good to have solid ground beneath my feet." When they'd finally arrived in Santa Cruz, he'd been startled by the change in the once sleepy island. It was now a bustling tourist destination. "What's happened to this village? Why is it like this when the rest of Tenerife seems to be flourishing?"

"Ask your grandfather that question." Lucia looked Rafe over, clinging to Tomas like she would never let him go, her chin up. "Are you ready to see him or do you wish to rest first? I have a guest room ready for you in the main house."

Rafe stayed where he was, not surprised by the woman's cold look. Nothing had changed here. He'd never felt welcome. The last time he'd seen the old man they'd exchanged bitter words and he'd left vowing never to come back. He still couldn't believe Matias had sent for him. He glanced around again. The clan obviously needed leadership but it wasn't his responsibility, damn it. He mentally braced himself for the coming meeting then nodded.

"Take me to the old man. I might as well get this over with." He winced when Tom slapped him on the back.

"That's the spirit. Face him like a man." Tom sighed. "Even sick as he is, I bet you a hundred euros that he has you begging to come back and serve him before you know it. Grandfather has always been a master manipulator."

Rafe had a feeling the bet was a good one. He'd run because his grandfather had terrified him. He'd known that if he'd stayed he would have spent eternity doing the old man's bidding and would have never become his own man. "Euros?"

"It's our currency now. You've been gone way too long, bro." Tom started to slap him on the back again but stopped at the look Rafe gave him. "Follow me. We've got Grandfather set up in a ground floor bedroom. He can't make the stairs to the master now."

"You're kidding." Rafe followed Tom into the main building. His grandfather had always ruled from his master suite. It featured a huge bed with carved animals that had frightened him when he'd been a small child. As he'd grown, he'd loved to hear the stories his grandfather had told about the mythological creatures pictured in the carvings. When Tom opened the door to what had been the study, the smell of medicine and urine hit him hard. He had to swallow to keep from gagging.

"Sorry, but he's lost control of some of his functions." Lucia hurried ahead of them. They heard a sharp slap and rapid Spanish. A servant girl with a red cheek hurried out with dirty linens, her head down. Lucia stuck her head out into the hall. "Give us a minute to clean him up."

"I can't--" Rafe stepped back toward the living room, at a loss. Five long minutes passed before he heard a voice he had never forgotten.

"Get the hell in here, boy."

Rafe stepped inside the darkened room. Lucia threw a fresh sheet over the wasted body in the narrow bed and hurried out. She patted Rafe's shoulder as she went by then whispered something to her husband.

"Uh, would you like to be left alone?" Tom sidled toward the door.

"Leave us." Grandfather didn't sound as weak as he looked, his once robust frame obviously down to skin and bones.

"Yes, sir." Tom stepped outside and closed the door.

"Do you want some fresh air?" Rafe didn't wait for an

answer, just walked over and pulled aside one of the heavy curtains and unlocked a window. He raised it a foot and took a deep breath. How could his grandfather stand it in here?

"Quit fussing and stand beside me where I can see you." The order was in a softer tone this time. "It's been a long time, Rafael."

"Yes, sir." Rafe moved to stand beside the bed. He looked down at the man who he remembered as strong, virile, and invincible. The change was shocking. Sallow face, sunken cheekbones and dark circles under his eyes, Grandfather looked like he didn't have long to live. Rafe swallowed and blinked, appalled to find that he was tearing up.

"Man up. You going to weep over me like a woman?" Grandfather coughed and sounded like he was strangling. Rafe looked around and found a carafe of water and empty glass nearby. He filled the glass and helped his grandfather sit up to drink. When the coughing fit subsided, he laid him back down and wiped his grandfather's streaming eyes with a tissue.

"Are you okay?" Rafe set the glass back down. They were speaking English. Which was a surprise. His grandfather usually lapsed into the Old Language, a mixture of Spanish and something else Rafe had never bothered to identify. He guessed the old man was trying to please him. No, not possible. Matias Castillo never pleased anyone but himself.

"What do you think?" Matias waved a thin hand. "Don't answer that. I know I look like shit. I'm dying, boy. Otherwise, I never would have sent for you. You made it clear more than a century ago that you don't want to be here." He cleared his throat. "It's a hell of a thing but I need you."

"Dying? How did this happen? Who did it?" Rafe pulled up a chair and sat. His knees were jelly. Seeing the old man like this... Matias had raised him, been more of a father to him than his own ever had. Yes, they'd had differences. It was what happened when two men with strong personalities tried to share a home.

"I have an idea." Matias managed a rueful smile. Silver whiskers and thinning gray hair. Another reason for Rafe to freak out. Shifters didn't go gray or lose their hair.

"Tell me. I will bring this man to justice. I swear it." Rafe laid his hand over his grandfather's. The fact that his skin was cool and thin as parchment made him try to will his own heat and vitality into it. "What do you know?"

"Poison is a woman's tool. And this started because of a woman." Grandfather's chuckle was rusty. "I always did have lusty urges, much to your grandmother's disgust and dismay. Shiloh is a beauty, belongs to the shifter clan that makes its base in Western Morocco." He sighed and closed his eyes. "Hot blooded. I never could resist..." He glanced at Rafe. "Tomas says you are involved with a were-cat. Is that true?"

"Yes. We're going to marry. She's carrying my children, three of them." Rafe dared his grandfather to start in on that.

"Children. Ah. You are a lusty lad too." A short bark of laughter that ended in another coughing fit was all the reaction Rafe got. "Well now. That can be good or bad. Depending on what she gives you. But you know that. You always did what you wanted, damn the consequences. Too much like me, Rafael. I'm sure this cat is a beauty. Eh?"

"Yes, she is." Rafe wanted to get back to why he'd been dragged here. "The poison, Grandfather. How--"

"How did it work on me? Damned if I know. We've sent men everywhere, looking for an antidote. There must be one. But so far, no luck." His dark eyes had sunk into his skull but they were sharp as ever. "Your children could be the future of this clan, Rafael."

"No, they couldn't." Rafe saw his grandfather's mouth tighten. He wasn't going to get into this now. "About this woman. Why would she poison you? What about

Grandmother? Is she all right?"

"Iliana is fine, just furious over the affair. It's not my first, of course, or even my hundredth. Your grandmother is used to my roving eye. She chooses to ignore it for the good of the clan. I'm discreet for the same reason. There have been many of these little itches that I have scratched. Usually a generous gift of jewelry or gold will see the thing finished with the other woman happy enough to go away quietly. But this time…"

"You picked the wrong woman." Rafe looked down at his own clenched fists. This was why he'd never married. Tying himself to Lacy meant he'd have to be faithful. Could he do it? Forever? The men in his family didn't have a good track record. He needed to decide that he could and would if he wanted to give his children a true family.

He'd grown up with a father who had sired children with several women because Rafe's mother had left the clan to return to her demon family. Tomas' mother was a clan beauty who had been one of his father's mistresses. Tomas had always tried to gain their father's attention without success. Finally Emiliano had decided he couldn't live without Rafe's beautiful demon mother and had abandoned his children and the clan forever. Rafe looked up at his grandfather's sigh.

"Of course she was wrong. I was blinded by her beauty. I kept the affair going when I should have left her, paid her off and moved on. But Shiloh became demanding. Yes, she liked her jewels, money. But she wanted more." Grandfather looked away, staring at the shelves full of books that filled his study. His antique desk had obviously been moved out to make room for the hospital bed he lay in.

"What, Grandfather?"

"She wanted me to put your grandmother aside and become my mate. Stupid bitch." He finally looked at Rafe. "I've been with your grandmother for millennia. We have always ruled our family and this clan together. I would never set Iliana aside." He started coughing again. "Some would say I deserve a lingering death for my sins."

Rafe didn't disagree. His grandfather's infidelities weren't news to him. He'd heard the gossip when he'd lived here. Instead of blasting the old man for failing to keep his cock in his pants, he stood. "Where is Grandmother? Maybe she finally decided enough is enough. You sure she didn't commission this poison herself?"

"Settle down, boy. Your grandmother would never jeopardize the clan by leaving it without a strong leader. I may be a 'faithless asshole', her words, but I do keep the clan strong."

"Do you? Why is this place looking like it was abandoned a century ago? I can't believe what I saw when we drove in. Obviously no one is overseeing the upkeep of the village. Are you having money trouble? Can't you afford to pay for repairs?" Rafe paced the length of the bed and back.

"Shut up. You have no idea how long I've been suffering. Now you exhaust me. Go see your grandmother. Ask her these questions. She took over when I couldn't. Did that make her happy, this woman who did nothing but nag me to pay attention to clan dealings? No. Instead, she left me and moved into a house at the other end of the village. Tomas can show you." He closed his eyes.

"You humiliated her with your affairs. Of course she left." Rafe thought about how Grandmother must feel. Making an open break with Grandfather would salvage her pride at least. "Have members of the clan taken sides? If you live, will there be a power struggle?" He could imagine it. If Grandmother could make the village prosperous again, why wouldn't the people follow her willingly?

"Leave me now. There will be no power struggle. If you don't help find a cure for this poison, I'm a dead man." He opened them again. "And think about this. I need you to stay in the village no matter what happens. It's time for you to take your place here. You said it. We need leadership. Your father won't leave his demon bride. Tomas is weak, led by his *pene*, his woman stronger than he is. So you, my boy, are going to have to lead this clan when I am gone. You must."

Rafe stared down at the old man who he had never expected to look older than thirty. He wanted to argue, shift out of there and take the next plane home. But instead he found himself looking around the room and remembering the years when this man had been the father he'd needed, the man who'd taught him to fight, to shift, to confront a mother who cared more for her fellow demons than she did for the child she kept leaving behind.

"Have you seen a doctor?"

"What good would that do? We're not human." Matias opened his eyes and shivered. "Shut the window before you leave. It's cold in here." He pulled the sheet up to his neck.

"There are doctors who work on paranormals. I know of some. I will send for one." Rafe walked over to shut the window, even though the heat in the room was stifling.

"Whatever you wish. It will do no good. I know my time is almost at an end." His grandfather closed his eyes.

Rafe found a blanket on a chest under the window and spread it over his grandfather.

"Don't give up, *Abuelo*." He couldn't help himself and squeezed Matias's foot. "We fight in this clan. You taught me that. I'll find out who did this and make sure you survive it. But then I'm leaving."

CHAPTER THREE

Lacy dragged herself out of bed after a sleepless night. Not that there had been much night left after her sister had driven her home. Now it was after two in the afternoon. No wonder she was starving. She sat for a moment on the side of the bed and felt the babies adjust to the new position. She could barely breathe these days. God, but she wondered how she could go another six weeks. The bathroom seemed a mile away but she had to get there. So she dragged herself to her feet and hurried, barely making it to the toilet. Relief.

Then she saw one of Rafe's socks on the floor. The tears she'd been holding back gave way and she grabbed a towel to hold against her face. Muffling her sobs, she leaned over, letting her grief and fear go. She had to. Feeling sorry for herself and worrying about Rafe weren't going to help anyone. She had to *do* something.

"I thought I heard you get up." Amy stood in the doorway. "Lace, please don't cry. I'm sure Rafe is safe with his family."

Lacy looked up then stretched out her hand. When her sister rushed to grab it, she felt better. Family. She knew the comfort her own could give her but had no idea what

Rafe had in store with his. He'd made it clear that leaving his "clan" as he called them years ago had been necessary but not why. That was all she'd ever been able to pry out of him. He'd never talked about going back. But he hadn't hesitated when his brother had asked him to come with him. Of course there'd been guns pointed at him as persuasion.

"He's strong, able to protect himself, and he didn't look scared. Yeah, you're right. I'm sure he'll be fine." She looked down at her swollen stomach which stretched her cotton nightgown to the limit. "He'll be frantic to get back here before the babies are born though. He's going to be a wonderful father."

"And husband. You *are* going to say yes when he gets back, aren't you?" Amy squeezed her fingers. "He loves you, Lace. Don't be stupid about this. He's over his Glory St. Clair fixation."

"I hope so." Lacy winced when Amy tightened her hold. "Okay, I know so. He loves me. I'll marry him. But first I'm going to find out who the hell ratted him out. Clearly Rafe hadn't wanted to be found by his clan. So there's a spy here in Austin who told his family his location. I want to know everything there is to know about this shifter clan and where they live. That spy is going to spill it all."

"Great. Let's go after him or her. You know who it is?" Amy helped Lacy stand.

"I have a good idea. Go make coffee and sandwiches while I take a shower. Decaf for me. And get out of here. I'm not a pretty sight naked though Rafe didn't seem to mind seeing me that way." Lacy held onto the glass shower door.

"And you doubted he loves you?" Amy laughed when Lacy threw a washcloth at her. It hit the floor. "Now I want to see you pick that up, cow."

"Bitch." Lacy realized her blue mood was lifting.

"We're cats, not dogs, Sis. I'm a queen and you know

it." With a hair flip, Amy shut the bathroom door.

Lacy laughed. Her sister had the knack of helping her see the bright side of things. And action would do even more. She turned on the water and stripped off her gown. No way could she pick up that washcloth so she got a fresh one from the bathroom closet. Cow? More like elephant. But, as the babies started a soccer game in her tummy, she realized it was a small price to pay for bringing Rafe's children into the world.

"Yes, I know where Rafe's clan lives. I'm one of his cousins. Didn't he tell you that?" Kira looked around the shop where they both worked. Vintage Vamp's Emporium on Austin's trendy Sixth Street was busy in the last few days before Christmas. She was tearing off tags and writing up a sale for a customer who was going through the display of sweaters nearby.

"No. But I heard you two talking in a foreign language. Tell me where his family lives. Have you been communicating with them?" Lacy grabbed Kira's arm. "Spying for them?"

"Excuse me?" Kira jerked her arm away. "Where's this coming from?"

"His brother came to my mother's place last night and took Rafe away. To see his ailing grandfather." Lacy was suddenly very aware of the mortals in the shop. She smiled and took a dress from a woman who emerged from the dressing room. As long as she was here, she was going to have to work. "How did it fit?"

"Perfect. I'm going to look for some earrings to go with it. Do you have some?" The woman noticed the jewelry case and pointed to a pair locked inside. "Those. I think those would look great."

"I'll help her." Amy stepped behind the counter. "Kira, you look a little, um, pale."

"Oh, give it up, girlfriend. I don't get pale." Kira had dark skin but she did look upset. "Did Tomas say what was wrong with Grandfather?"

"We can't get into it here." Lacy knew they had to keep the store open. It was Glory's shop and they'd promised to hold down the fort while she was on her honeymoon. "What I want to know is if you're the one who told Tomas that Rafe was here and how to find him."

"You really think I spied on him? For the clan?" Kira drew herself up to her full height, which was an awesome six feet without the four inch platforms she wore today. "I didn't." She turned away to take the sweater the customer handed her and switched on a smile as she added up the total and took the woman's credit card. Before either Lacy or Kira spoke to each other again, Kira finished her sale and wished the customer a Merry Christmas.

"Then who could it be?" Lacy sagged onto the stool in front of the counter. "Who else would know the family and report to them?"

"I have a suspicion." Kira waved her hand around the packed shop. "Seriously, we can't do this now. Every dressing room is full and I've got a customer waving at me from the locked case with the vintage handbags." She grabbed a key ring. "I know you don't feel like working, hon. You're puffing like a beached whale."

Amy looked up. "She's right, Lace. You don't look so good. Go home, put your feet up."

"Not a chance." Lacy narrowed her gaze as she watched Kira help a customer select a Gucci bag. "I'm getting a name before I leave here. Do you believe Kira? She and Rafe share a grandfather. Why wouldn't she send messages home?"

"Maybe she left for the same reason Rafe did. He didn't tell you what it was?" Amy smiled and took the earrings the customer selected. "Did you see the matching bracelet? I think it would be a wonderful Christmas gift to yourself." She winked at Lacy. "I always buy myself something when I'm shopping for others."

"Let me see it. And that other bracelet, the sterling

bangle. You two are sisters, aren't you? That red hair is a dead giveaway." The customer patted Lacy on the shoulder. "Do what she says, girl, and go home and put your feet up. When's your due date?"

"February first, but I'm thinking these babies want to come sooner. I'm having triplets." Lacy rubbed her stomach. Her maternity sweater was showing signs of strain too. She'd be glad when she could get into decent clothes again.

"Multiples? Honey, they always come early. I had twins and they were six weeks early. But my preemies were perfect. You should see them now. Five year old terrors." She pulled out a cell phone and showed a picture of blond twin boys. "We have great support group for mothers of multiples. You should come after you give birth and things settle down a little. We get together and vent. Make our men babysit so we can have some 'me' time." She dug a card out of her purse. "Call me when you're ready."

Lacy tried to read the card but it blurred as she realized what the woman had said. "Early? They could come early? I don't know whether to pray for that or not. My fiancé is out of town." Lacy bit her lip. Fiancé. Yes, she was calling Rafe that. She wished he'd left the ring here. If he had, she'd have it on her finger right now.

"I'm sure he'll be back in time. That group sounds great. She'll come. I can babysit if Rafe is busy when you meet. He owns N-V, that cool club down the street. Have you been there?" Amy kept chattering away while she wrapped the jewelry the customer had selected. She'd taken the clerking job at the store for the holidays but Lacy hoped she'd stay on while Glory was gone. They were already short-handed and Lacy was planning to take some time off after the babies were born. Amy could fill in for her. If she went into labor early... Oh, the complications were endless.

"Of course. We meet there sometimes. Great cocktails." The woman whipped out a credit card. "Good luck. Hope your man is home soon."

"Me, too." Lacy blinked and refused to let a tear fall.

Kira appeared with the vintage Gucci purse then grabbed one of Lacy's hands. "Ed. The accountant who works for Rafe at his club. He and I have dated a few times and I know he has ties to the clan too. He's the only one I can think of who might have reported to them." She stepped around the counter and hugged Lacy. "He's a decent guy, Lacy. If he did it, I'm sure he had a good reason."

"Like what?" Lacy was aware of the many mortals crowded around them. "Three of you from the same, um, family show up in the same Texas town, miles away from home. Which is where exactly?"

"Across the Atlantic. An island off the coast of Spain. One I'm sure you've never heard of." Kira turned when her customer asked for some help. "Be right there. Listen, go see Ed. I'm sure he's working at the club tonight. If you get answers, I'd like to know what they are too."

"Off the coast of Spain? Thanks for telling me that much at least." Lacy knew she sounded bitter as she heaved herself to her feet. "I'll get out of your way." She smiled at the customers anxious to get their sales completed. "Merry Christmas, everyone. Thanks for shopping at Vintage Vamp's."

"Where are you going? Surely not to the club. You need to rest." Amy couldn't leave the counter while she waited for the credit card to go through.

"I have to go to Rafe's club. Someone has to tell them he's going to be gone for a while. I guess it's me. And I want to talk to Ed." Lacy stopped next to the door as a new customer rushed inside. A cold front had blown in and the air was crisp, much colder than it had been at the wedding the night before.

"Remember, Ed is a decent guy, Lacy. Don't go all, um, wildcat on him." Kira smiled, like she was joking, but Lacy got the message.

"I'll do what I need to. I'm going to get answers, one way or another." Lacy pulled her black wool cape, the only thing big enough to go around her these days, tight and hurried out the door. She walked down Sixth Street, glad that it was almost dark. The club wasn't open during the day but there was a happy hour that should be starting about now. It was only a few blocks down the street but by the time she saw the neon sign that said "N-V", she was out of breath and wondering if the babies were about to fall out on their own. It would almost be a relief.

Ed wasn't at the door, which was sometimes his duty, but the man there waved her in. As Rafe's lady, she was always welcome. Lacy looked around and saw that the bar and the free "build your own nachos" buffet were doing a lively business. Nachos. She could go for some of those. She headed over, loaded a plate and caught the bartender's eye. He brought her the usual--a glass of milk--and settled her at a quiet table away from the singles scene ramping up at the bar.

"You happen to know where I could find Ed?" Lacy shoveled in a loaded nacho and sighed in contentment. The babies were used to spicy food. She'd had cravings for chips, jalapenos and bean dip for a solid month.

"He's in back working on the books. You want me to send for him?"

"Thanks. I need to talk to him. If you don't mind." Lacy took a gulp of milk. Her stomach gurgled and she wondered if she should switch to water.

"No problem." The bartender hurried back to the bar and picked up the phone there.

Lacy had polished off the nachos and milk and was thinking about asking for a bottle of water when Ed came out from the office tucked under the balcony nearby. The club had been carved out of a vintage building with several floors. The high ceilings made for great acoustics and the disc jockey had cranked up the music for the bar crowd. Lacy wished she could tell him to dial it down. Her head was pounding and the nachos weren't settling like they usually did.

Ed was big, dark and dangerous looking. It was a great look when he was on door duty and needed to discourage a bad element from entering the club. He was also a brilliant accountant and, to quote Kira, a nice guy. His hobby of dressing as Aretha Franklin and doing a killer "Chain of Fools" only made him more interesting. The fact that he was a shape-shifter who liked to shift into a gorilla just added to his resume. Rafe had talked about making Ed his assistant manager. Damn it.

"Hey. Where's the boss man?" He sat across from her when Lacy gestured.

"Gone. His brother came last night and strong-armed him into returning to his family. You know anything about that?" Lacy didn't miss the slight tightening around Ed's lips. She leaned forward. "You do! You sack of shit. You've been spying on him." Her fingernails morphed into claws which dug into the wooden tabletop.

"Calm down, Lacy. I admit I may have sent a message or two back to Matias. It was my duty." Ed leaned back but not quite out of reach.

"Fuck that. Rafe gave you a good job here. Responsibilities. He *trusted* you, Ed." Lacy's voice broke even while she grabbed his arm and held onto it. He didn't wince. She had to give him points for that, but she knew her claws were drawing blood. He glanced around to make sure no one was paying attention to them.

"You want to take this to Rafe's office?"

"Why? So you can go gorilla on my ass? No thank you. We'll stay right here where I have witnesses." Lacy released him but made sure he knew she wasn't going to let him leave the table. "If I have to shift in front of a room full of mortals, I sure as hell will. I want answers and I want them now."

"Now you know you're not going to do that. Just calm down. I do appreciate him and all he's done for me. I promise you, he's not in danger, Lacy." Ed's calm voice made her want to scratch a path down his lean cheeks.

"Don't you dare try to humor me! Why did you tell the people in this clan Rafe belongs to how to find him? Seems like if he wanted to communicate with those folks, he would have. And now, when he's about to become a father, they've dragged him off to God knows where. Because of your spying!" Lacy felt on the verge of tears but sucked them back. No way was she crying.

"I did what I had to do. For Matias, that's Rafe's grandfather. I owed him. There aren't that many shifters left. This is about the survival of the clan." Ed leaned closer, his voice soft. Of course Lacy could hear him, even though the music was loud and the customers crowding the bar were getting raucous as they hit hard the three dollar Margarita special.

"You and Kira are dark, Rafe is white. Are you all three part of the same clan? And you didn't answer my question. Why, Ed? Rafe broke ties with his family. You should have asked him if he wanted to be found." Lacy picked up a paper napkin and blotted her cheeks. Damned pregnancy hormones. She didn't cry. She sniffed and shot him a look that made him sit back and widen his eyes. That was better. She wasn't going to shed one more damned tear.

"Kira and I come from an offshoot of the clan in North Africa. She's a cousin to Rafe, I am not." Ed ran a hand through his short hair. "Shit. None of that matters. I did what I had to do. I respect Rafe, I do. You're right. He's been good to me since I came to this town. I owe him. But I wouldn't have come to Austin at all if not for an obligation I owed to Matias. The man saved my father's life a long time ago. He can call in a favor and I must do as he wills. It's clan law. I can't refuse. So I came here and began to report to Matias about his grandson. I am not proud to spy as you call it. I count Rafe as a friend now. It makes me sick to betray his trust."

"This is bullshit." Lacy rubbed her stomach. Those

nachos. The gas pains were getting worse. She was swearing off spicy food as of now. She dug in her purse for a Tums and chewed.

Ed frowned at her. "As a cat, I know you understand family loyalty."

"Sure. But you're going to help *me* now. Because you were disloyal to Rafe. First you need to figure out who can run this club while the boss is gone." She held up her hand when Ed opened his mouth. "It can't be you. You're taking me to this clan's island. I have to follow Rafe so I can be there with him. His brother said his grandfather is dying. If the worst happens and the old man dies, I should be there to comfort my man." She gasped when another pain hit her. She popped another antacid. "Second, I need to know why they took Rafe at gunpoint. What's the story there? Seems a little extreme to me."

"Matias has always favored Rafe. He probably hopes he'll stay and lead the clan when he dies."

"Stay on some island in the middle of nowhere?" Lacy wondered if she knew Rafe at all. But focusing on her love life was beyond her at the moment. She looked down at her stomach which seemed to have developed a life of its own as it twisted, turned and threatened to tear her apart from the inside out.

"It's beautiful there. You'd like it, I'm sure. It's become a big tourist spot now." Ed actually smiled, selling the place.

Lacy wanted to smack him.

"I'm not sure what exactly happened that made Rafe take off all those years ago, but I guess his grandfather felt that he had to force a face to face. So he could try to persuade him to come home permanently." Ed frowned when Lacy hissed and reared back in her chair. "Hey, are you all right?"

"No, I'm not all right." Lacy stood and looked back at the wet vinyl seat. She couldn't ignore what was happening another minute. Could the timing be any worse? She wasn't ready. She looked at Ed's kind eyes and wanted to slap him just because he was there and Rafe wasn't.

"Lacy?" Ed stood next to her now, his hand on her elbow.

"My water just broke. Ready or not, I'm having these babies." Lacy gasped when a pain ripped through her. "Get me out of here. Now."

CHAPTER FOUR

"What should we do? Who should I call?" Ed grabbed her elbow. "Do cats go to a hospital or…" He seemed at a loss for words.

"Normally I'd have these babies at home, with my mother and grandmother as midwives." Lacy doubled over when the first real contraction hit hard. She held on to the table top again, scoring it with her claws. Pant, that's what she'd been taught to do as soon as she'd told her mother she was pregnant. There were other things, lessons mothers passed on to their daughters. Were-cats delivered easily. But these weren't babies fathered by a cat. Lacy trembled as the pain finally subsided. She couldn't sit in that wet seat and this wasn't feeling easy. At all.

"Normally." Ed grabbed her purse and pulled out her cell. "I'm calling your mother. I see her name here on your contact list."

"Wait! I don't think…" Lacy wanted Rafe, no one else. "Coast of Spain." She took a shuddery breath. "How isolated is this clan enclave. Can he get here fast?" She saw Ed shake his head. "Then call my doctor. Ian MacDonald. Get him on the phone." Her legs were shaking as another pain ripped across her middle. Too fast. Too close together. This wasn't right. Maybe she did want her mother and Amy. But she'd be damned if she squat over some ancient birthing stool like the tradition demanded with the female cats howling in sympathy around her.

Ed was on the phone. "She says her water broke and I can see she's in pain." He passed the phone to Lacy. She just shook her head, afraid to let go of the table or she'd howl the place down. "Uh, just a minute. She's not able to talk right now. Maybe you should come here." He listened but kept his eyes on Lacy. "I'll see what I can do. Yeah, I'll call you back if we can't." He ended the call.

Lacy staggered over to a clean chair and finally sat down again. The pain had eased. "What did he say?" She reached for the phone and found Amy's number.

"He wants you to come to him. He has facilities that are sterile and equipment that will be better for the babies, he says. He wants me to remind you that these are preemies."

"As if I'm not already freaking out about that." Lacy hit Amy's number. "Sis, I need you. Get your car and drive over to Rafe's club. I'm, hah, hah, hah, having the babies. Right now." Ed grabbed her phone while she leaned over and gave into another pain. God but this hurt. She'd read . . . Oh she couldn't focus on what the hell she'd read as she rode a wave of pain so bad she bit through her lip and tasted blood. Rafe. He should be here. Damn his family. If she ever met any of them she'd let them know they were on her permanent shit list.

"Forget that. I've got a big SUV. I can lay the back seats flat and Lacy can ride there." He frowned as he held her phone to his ear. "Yeah, yeah. I heard what she told you. This is Ed. I'm not leaving her alone. But she wants you too. Maybe you should call your mother. Tell her to meet us at Ian MacDonald's." He held the phone away from his ear. "Look, lady, MacDonald was Lacy's choice. Not mine."

"Give me that." Lacy grabbed the phone. "Do what Ed

says. This freaking hurts! I'm not letting Mama deliver these babies naturally like cats have for centuries, you hear me? I want modern medicine. Pain killers! Call her or not, I don't give a damn. Now Ed's going to load me in his car. Hurry and get your butt down here so I have someone to scream at when the next contraction hits. Got it?"

"I'm on my way." Amy sounded out of breath. "I hit the door the minute you said you were in labor. Hang up so I can call Mom."

"She's going to go nuts." Lacy's eyes filled with tears and she caught herself before she sobbed. No, she had to suck it up. "But these babies are half shifter. Ian warned me they might be due sooner than I thought. I figured he was thinking we had the same gestation period as regular cats. Idiot vampire. " Lacy started to laugh then got caught by another pain. "Aw shit." She threw the phone at Ed and leaned over, her hands on her knees. A few mortals at the bar had noticed what was going on with her. Ed waved at the bartender and tossed him his car keys.

"Get my car and bring it around front. This lady is having her babies right now." He nodded to the crowd at the bar. "Dollar tequila shots on me in honor of the boss. These are his babies!" He pointed to Lacy's swollen stomach. She rolled her eyes as a cheer went up and everyone turned to the harried bartender who quickly threw Ed's keys to a busboy with whispered instructions.

"Can you walk or do you want me to carry you?" Ed frowned down at her.

Lacy was sure her face was red and she pushed back her damp hair with a shaky hand. The pain had eased. Ed was a giant of a man but she didn't think he'd be up for carrying her. She was no lightweight even when she wasn't carrying a trio of children in her belly. She staggered to her feet, holding onto his arm.

"I'll try to walk but no guarantees. Be ready to catch me if I--"

"Screw it." Ed scooped her up into his arms, only

staggering slightly under her weight. A round of applause broke out from the bar patrons, along with some whistles and shout outs.

"Careful. You drop me and your job will be history." Lacy managed a wave toward the bar then held onto Ed's massive shoulders. No pain for the moment. A blessing. One of the women from the bar crowd brought her a bottle of water.

"Drink, honey. It'll help. I saw you chowing down on nachos earlier. You sure this is labor and not gas?" She patted Lacy's stomach.

Lacy took the water and gulped some of it down. It was cold and refreshing. "Thanks, but my water broke. No question. This is it." Why the hell did people think it was okay to touch her stomach just because she was pregnant? It was an invasion of her privacy that she'd never gotten used to. Too bad they always said something nice. She was on the edge of slapping away the woman's hand and yelling "Fuck off!" when a new pain distracted her and she gasped.

"Oh. Good luck." The woman hurried back to her crew, telling everyone the news. This seemed to call for another round of dollar shots and everyone was toasting the babies as Lacy and Ed hit the door to outside.

The icy wind hit Lacy's wet skirt and made her shiver while she panted her way through a contraction. Ed's hot shifter body next to hers helped keep her warm but did nothing for the pain ripping her apart. It was easing when his black SUV arrived at the curb. He gave quick instructions to the bus boy and the back seats were down and ready for her in less than the time it took for Amy to arrive at a dead run.

"Oh, my God, look at you! Where's your cape?" Amy glared at Ed. "She's freezing. Are you just going to lay her down on that hard carpet in the back of the car?"

"I didn't think--" Ed sat Lacy down on the tailgate.

"Obviously." Amy grabbed the busboy standing next to

the door into the club just enjoying the show. "Go get my sister's cape. It must be where she was sitting inside. Bring it and any blankets you have in there out to us. And hurry." She shook her head. "Lace! You should have told me your skirt was wet. I could have brought you a fresh one from the shop."

"Shut up, Amy." Lacy bent over as a fresh contraction hit her hard. "I don't give a shit about the hard carpet. Just help me get out of this wind. Ed, slide me inside and shut the tailgate. I can feel heat coming from inside the car. Please hurry. This is going way faster than the books said it should." Lacy panted as Ed gently knelt beside her and eased her in so she could lie back. She kept her knees up until the pain finally seemed to have run its course. "Amy?"

"I'm here, Sis. Forget the books. Those were written for regular people. You, my dear sister, are anything but regular and these babies will come out when they want to and how they want to." Amy crawled in and sat next to her.

Lacy gave her sister an evil look. "Is that meant to be comforting? What the hell?"

Amy flushed. "Uh, I don't know. Maybe. I admit I'm out of my depth here. Looking at you suffering is making me think a vow of celibacy is in my future." She grimaced then grabbed something. "Just in time. Your cape. Let me cover you with it."

"Thanks. I'm sorry I yelled at you. I'm just hurting so bad." Lacy grabbed Amy's hand and squeezed, gently she hoped. But when Amy squealed she let her go. This pain was worse than anything she'd ever felt before. No wonder she was going out of her mind with it. Lacy closed her eyes then realized something. "Ed, why aren't we moving yet?" She sat up on her elbows. "Someone shut that freaking back door!" It slammed instantly.

"I was waiting for you to be ready to go. Can you tell me where Ian MacDonald lives?" Ed sat in the driver's seat but hadn't put the car in drive yet. "Give me an address and I can use the GPS to get us there. I'll hurry but I need something to go by."

Lacy stammered out the address then lay back and closed her eyes. Amy's hand landed on hers, prying the water bottle out of her hand. She'd managed to splash her sweater. Fantastic. Wet from top to bottom.

"Have you tried to call Rafe? He should know what's going on. Maybe he can get here in time to see the babies born." Amy smoothed Lacy's hair back from her face.

"No, he's too far away. If I tell him now it will just frustrate him. When the babies are safely here, I'll do Face Time with him, show him the babies. Until then..." Tears again. Stupid hormones totally out of whack. But she wanted Rafe holding her hand. *Needed* him.

"Until then you've got me. And Mom is on her way to Ian's. I didn't know where he lives either but she said she'd figure it out. Guess she knows someone who knows someone." Amy shrugged. "That's our mother."

"She's going to fight Ian for this birth. Help me with her, Amy. Ian knows what he's doing. Remember, he did an ultrasound of the babies early on. I trust him." Lacy moaned when they hit a bump. Clearly Ed was driving fast. But Ian lived away from the city in a hilltop home that was a good thirty minute drive if you were careful. There were winding roads and... Well, she'd just have to hope Ed knew what he was doing. Lying down had helped and for the moment the pains had stopped. Was that good or bad? She held onto Amy's hand and waited. To her surprise, she felt sleep pulling at her. Tempting. If she could sleep through childbirth, how cool would that be?

CHAPTER FIVE

"I can't come to your shifter clan, Valdez. I'm busy delivering your children." Ian MacDonald sounded like he was having the time of his life.

"What?" Rafe stared at the phone. It had taken way too long to get an international connection. Now Ian was toying with him.

"You heard me. Lacy went into labor early. She's here now, about to deliver. I don't know where your clan is located, but I assume you won't be able to get here in time to be in on the big event." Ian actually chuckled. "Too bad. She could use your support. Her mother is being a real pain in the ass."

"If you're lying…"

"Here, I'll put her on the phone. Lacy, not her mother."

"Rafe, is it really you?" Lacy sounded exhausted.

"Baby? Are you in labor? For real?" Rafe wanted to shift and head across the Atlantic. Too bad he knew it would be stupid and suicidal.

"Yes. I wish you were here." She sounded out of breath. "This hurts like a son of a bitch."

"If I could be there, I would. How much longer will it

take? Maybe I can make it. The clan has its own plane." Rafe looked around to see if he could grab someone to make the arrangements, but he was alone in the living room.

"You can't. Ian says within the hour." Lacy squealed. "Oh, God, I want to push. Ian says not yet. He's going to give me an epidural in a minute or two so I won't feel anything after that. My mother is dead set against it but Amy's here with me. We're not letting Mama interfere."

"An hour. No, I can't make it. Damn, I'm sorry, Lace. I wanted..." Rafe bowed his head, staring down at his black dress shoes. Hell, he didn't even have a change of clothes here. He had so much to do, but fuck that. He wanted to be in Austin, holding Lacy's hand, helping her through this. And to be there to see his children come into the world.

"I know, Rafe. You weren't given a choice. Not with guns aimed at you." Lacy moaned. "I just wish..."

"No more than I do, baby. You be sure to get those painkillers. No reason to suffer any more than you already have. Can you put us on Face Time? So I can see you?" Rafe gripped the phone hard.

"No, I'm a mess. Wait and see us afterwards. When the babies are here. We have the names figured out. Right? Unless you've second thoughts. Now that you're back with the clan?" Lacy's voice cracked. "Tell me your thoughts. Are you okay? Did they hurt you? What about your grandfather?"

"He's not doing well. That's why I called Ian. He needs a doctor. Here, they don't believe in them. Like your mother doesn't. You understand. They cling to the old ways."

"Too well. Amy's ready to tie Mama to a chair so she'll let Ian do his thing. But what about you? Are you all right?" Lacy moaned again.

"I'm fine except that I hate like hell not being with you right now. I hear you moaning. I'm hanging up so you can let go and scream that place down. I love you. Remember that. Okay?"

"Love you too."

"Now hand the phone to Ian."

"Here he is."

"Ian here. She's doing well. I'm going to give her something for the pain now." Ian sounded sure of himself.

"You'd better. I don't want her to suffer. If," Rafe cleared his throat. "If there's a choice between Lacy or the babies, Lacy is to be saved. Is that clear?"

"Relax, Valdez. They will all be fine. You're getting way too dramatic. Did you watch a sappy in-flight movie or something? I won't let anything happen to any of them. But if you want to name one of the boys Ian, I won't object." His laugh was the last thing Rafe heard as the line went dead.

"Trouble at home?" The soft feminine voice came from beside him on the worn leather couch in his grandfather's living room.

"Grandmother. I didn't hear you come in." Rafe stuck the phone in his jacket pocket. He did need to see about different clothes.

"I know you didn't. Your phone call clearly had all your attention." Iliana rested her hand on his leg. "You look worried."

"My lady is in labor. She's carrying triplets. My children. I should be there with her. Not here trying to solve a problem I know nothing about." Rafe saw his grandmother bite her lip and glance away from him. "I'm sorry. I want to help save Grandfather. Clearly he's dying."

"Sometimes I wish he *would* die. He's humiliated me time and again with his philandering ways." She faced Rafe and her eyes glittered with unshed tears. "This is only what he deserves for following his wandering eye. This time he chose a woman who had her own agenda. If only he had come to me and told me what she wanted!" She glanced back at the closed door to the study.

"And what would that have accomplished?" Rafe couldn't imagine that conversation.

His grandmother shocked him with a swear word in the old language. "I would have given him my blessing. Go with your whore, Matias! Let her have this clan if she wants it!" She lost her fire quickly and stared down at her fingers twisting together in her lap. "Why could I never be enough for him, Rafael?"

Rafe pulled his grandmother into his arms. "You know I have no answer for that, *Abuela*. Grandfather obviously has a flaw in his makeup. It may be a fatal flaw." He held her while she sobbed against his chest. It wasn't like her to show a woman's tender emotions. When he'd been growing up she'd been stern and in charge, taking over the daily running of the family when Matias had been away on one of his "missions". Rafe had been told Grandfather had enemies and often left to settle scores with other clans. Lies told to cover up the man's infidelities? He felt the respect he'd had for the old man disappear.

"It may be *my* fatal flaw that I still love him. Do you think we can save him, Rafael?" She sat back and wiped her eyes with a linen handkerchief.

"We can certainly try." Rafe had to admire her. Her loyalty was amazing even if his grandfather didn't deserve it.

"I know you want to leave. Who could blame you? Matias thinks you should take over the clan when he's gone. Chauvinist bastard. What have *I* been doing for a millennia? I lead this clan while he follows his cock to the nearest welcoming--"

"*Abuela*! I think I've heard enough about Grandfather and his unfaithfulness." Rafe laid his hand over hers. "Of course you should lead the clan. I have no interest in doing so. My family and home are in Texas. It's where I'll go once this poison business is settled. One way or another."

"Even if Matias dies, we must bring the poisoner to justice. You know?" Grandmother's shoulders were back, her chin up. She was tiny, always had been. But her spirit made her seem six feet tall and powerful. Rafe never wanted to tangle with her and knew why his grandfather had done his best to hide his affairs.

"First, I'm bringing a doctor here. There's one in Austin but he's busy. So I'm going to call another. He lives in Scotland. Closer to us and just as talented. In fact, he's interested in chemistry so he may be able to come up with an antidote. Did you figure out what Grandfather ate or drank that made him ill? Do you have any of the poison left?" Rafe pulled out his phone and went through the contact list. He couldn't call Jeremy Blade on his honeymoon, though he would certainly have the number he needed.

For a moment he waited to see if the familiar pain of jealousy hit him. Blade with Gloriana. No. His mind was too full of Lacy, laboring to bring their children into the world. It was good to know he'd left his passion for Glory behind and his priorities were in order. He would never want to be like his grandfather, a man who didn't know how to remain faithful to one woman. He finally found a number that would be useful and hit speed dial. His grandmother had rushed out of the room. He hoped to bring him some useful evidence.

"Hello." The woman sounded sleepy.

Rafe had no idea where she was or what time it was there. Honestly? He didn't care. "Caitlin? This is Rafe Valdez, Glory's friend." Caitlin Campbell was Jeremy Blade's sister. Last he knew, she was having an affair with the Scottish doctor he needed to reach.

"Ah, yes. Rafe. How are you?" Caitlin was waking up fast. "I'm sorry, I've been on a jet. Flew back from the wedding right afterwards and jet lag caught up with me."

"I've been better. But that's not important. Do you happen to have Dr. O'Connor with you?"

"Bart? Yes, he's right here. You may remember he was with me at the wedding." She said something to another person in the room. "Here he is. I hope someone isn't ill."

"Afraid so. Thanks, Caitlin." Rafe waited until he heard the definitely Scottish brogue of Dr. Bartholomew O'Connor on the line.

"Rafe. What's this Caitlin's telling me? Who's ill?"

"My grandfather. He's been poisoned. I seem to remember you're quite the expert on all things to do with chemistry."

"Well, yes. I've studied it for years. Any idea what he took or was given to him?" Bart sounded alert now, interested.

"No idea. I'm afraid Matias is too weak to move. Can you come to us?" Rafe told him how to get to the compound. "I could send a jet for you."

"No need. We just got home and haven't released the one we chartered. Cait and I were talking about taking another little trip and were giving ourselves a night or two here before we made a decision about where. Can I bring her along? Or is this a secret enclave?"

Rafe thought about it. "Bring her. And as much of your equipment as you think you'll need. I will see what I can find out before you get here. I'm trying to run down the poisoner. If I can get them to admit what they used, I'm sure that will help."

"Of course. In the meantime, try to build up the victim. Light broth, fluids if he can keep them down. Is he still lucid?"

"Yes." Rafe felt Grandmother's presence next to him again. "But he's very weak."

"I'm leaving here in two hours. That's how long it will take to get my things together. See you as soon as may be. Lucid is good news. Take heart, fellow." The call ended.

"You trust this man?" Grandmother handed Rafe a bottle. "This is what Matias was drinking when he fell ill. No one else has touched it. There is still some in the bottle. Not much but maybe…"

"Yes, that will help." Rafe pulled his grandmother

close. "He said lucid is good. We should try to get Grandfather to drink liquids, sip some broth. Hydrate him. Can you see to it?"

"What are you going to do?" She patted his chest then pulled away.

"Gather a force and go see this bitch Grandfather got entangled with. If there is any chance she's the one who did this, then I'm going to find out the truth. Even if I have to torture it out of her." Rafe strode out of the room.

He stopped in the central courtyard and looked around the village. A force? Did one exist in this pitiful excuse for a clan? He leapt onto the low brick in the center and rang the bell they used for emergencies. It had been there as long as he could remember. Luckily it still worked and people came streaming out of their houses. When the stream became a trickle he counted heads. Less than a hundred. It was pitiful. He had thought they numbered closer to a thousand. Where had everyone gone? Were they like him? Tired of the old ways and determined to make a new life without restrictions? He wouldn't be surprised.

"People of Clan Castillo. We have been attacked. The poisoning of Matias is as direct an assault on our clan as if an army had appeared at the gates. What are we going to do about it?" Rafe waited while there were rumblings and a few shouts. "Let me tell you what I want to do."

"Who put you in charge?" This from a man who was one of the few Rafe recognized. A crony of his grandfather's.

"Do you want to take over leadership, Miguel? If so, where have you been? Why are the houses in poor repair? Why is a burned out shell sitting there, a blight on the village square?" Rafe stared at the man until he bowed his head.

"I have my own problems. Too many children to feed and a nagging wife." That earned Miguel a cuff on the head from a woman who had a mean right hook.

"Then is there anyone else who wants to lead the village? Make a decision? Besides my grandmother? I know who keeps this village together. You would do well to support her from now on." Rafe scanned the crowd. No one wanted to make eye contact. "All right then. Here's what I propose. We need a dozen men or women who aren't afraid to fight to go with me across the water to see the woman who may have poisoned Matias. I want to get the truth out of her. If she is indeed the one who did this, we will try to see if there's an antidote and bring it back here before it is too late. Of course we will make sure she is punished as well. Who's with me?"

"I am!" Tomas hurried to stand next to Rafe on the wall. "Come on, fellows. This is a chance to shift. Show the people over there that we're not a dying clan brought low by a jealous bitch but shifters who have the guts to fight for what's right."

"Well said, brother." Rafe slapped Tomas on the back. Too bad his brother ruined it by falling off the wall and onto the nearest prickly bush. His curses made the crowd laugh but got some of the other men to step forward. Soon they had ten volunteers ready to go, four of them women.

"I'm glad someone is finally doing something. It seemed like we were just waiting for Matias to die." One of the women tied a headband around her wild blond hair. "This is what the clan needed, action. It's been too long since we've done anything but sit around and watch the village wither away."

"What do we have for weapons besides what Tomas shoved in my face when he dragged me here?" Rafe waited but no one said anything. "Are you kidding me? You think the other clan doesn't have any?" He saw his grandmother make her way through the crowd. She had a purse with her.

"Here is my credit card. Buy whatever you need. Just remember that you'll be shifting. If you fight against these people, send someone in to spy first. To see what you'll be up against." Her mouth was tight. "There's a boat in the harbor that you can take to their headquarters. Its name is," she swallowed. "*No Reglas*."

"No Rules." Rafe nodded. "That was obviously Grandfather's mantra. I'm sorry, Grandmother. But thank you. Is it large enough for this many of us?"

"It's the size of your grandfather's ego, Rafael." She looked at their band of fighters. "Plenty large enough to hold more than this crew." She sighed and glanced around, seeming to really see the disrepair and the sad numbers of the clan. "Your grandfather spared no expense when it came to his pleasure. That is why the village looks as it does. These past decades he cared nothing for us, but only for what he could get elsewhere. From now on things will be different. I will see to it." She turned on her heel and marched out of the square, the eyes of the crowd following her. A few of the women cheered but were quickly hushed with reminders that Matias was surely dying.

"She is a brave woman." Marguerite, a tall, bronzed brunette spat on the ground. "I wouldn't blame her if she herself poisoned Matias. He has been a poor husband to her."

"Iliana would never go so far." Miguel glanced at Rafe and Tomas. "But put a knife to his *pene*? I surely expected it, especially when he boasted about this latest whore of his in the tavern late at night. He made no secret of their affair. A wife shouldn't have dirty linen dragged home like that."

"Aye. I would have shoved Arturo's balls down his throat if I'd heard he was bragging about some *puta* to the men here." A petite blond pulled a knife from her boot. "You think I wouldn't? Ask him about the scar on his thigh."

The other men laughed uneasily. Arturo himself wrapped his arm around her. "You ask if we can fight with you, Rafael? This woman is ten times the fighter that many of the men are. I can attest to that. Chiquita, I'm hot just thinking about how I got that scar. When do we leave for the boat, Rafael?"

"Provisions and weapons first. Tomas and I will get the weapons in Santa Cruz. Can any of you shoot?" Rafe was relieved to see all hands go up.

"We are not novices, Rafael. None of us is young. Buy us good guns. We have knives at home, except for Chica here. She carries one on her at all times. It keeps me on my best behavior" Arturo grinned and looked around. He got nods of agreement.

"I'll handle provisions if you'd like, Rafael. Just tell me when you want to leave." Marguerite stepped forward.

"We go day after tomorrow. That will give me time to consult with the doctor I sent for. I hope he can find a cure for Matias. So get ready." They all nodded and strode away.

"Well done, brother." Tomas had stayed on the ground and reached up to help him down off the wall. "I heard your babies are being born as we speak. I apologize for pulling you away from that."

"Thanks." Rafe dragged a hand through his hair. He was desperate to call Lacy and see how she was. How the babies were. He also needed a hot shower. As if they had a line to each other, his phone buzzed in his pocket. He pulled it out and saw it was her.

"Lace? How are you?"

"Alive. Ripped apart. Sewn back together. We have two boys and a girl, Rafe. Gabriel, Lucas and Daniela. Those names still okay with you?"

"Sure, I guess." Rafe took a breath not sure he wasn't going to pass out. Holy shit. He was a father. "Tell me about them." He could hear them crying. "What's the matter with them? Why are they crying?"

"Who knows? Hungry maybe. Mad at being out of their nice warm womb. I don't know. But they're beautiful, Rafe, even if they are a little red, from all the screaming.

Ian's been great. Gave me the shot toward the end and I didn't feel much of anything."

"Two sons and a daughter. We did it. Well, I guess you did it. I'm so sorry I wasn't there to hold your hand or do whatever the hell fathers do during childbirth." Rafe felt the sting of tears and sat on the brick wall. Tomas's hand landed on his back.

"Blessings on them." His brother walked away, probably to spread the news.

"I'd probably have cursed you for putting me through this." She sighed. "But it was so worth it. It's amazing, Rafe. Three tiny human looking beings we created together. Can you believe it?"

"Not really. You sure you're okay? That must have been hard." Rafe realized his voice sounded thick. Yeah, like he was talking past a lump the size of an SUV.

"It was. Especially since you weren't here. But I survived. I had my sister and Ian. My mom even calmed down enough to help. Any news there?" She sounded as if she cared. What a woman.

"We're working on finding out what poison Matias took. I sent for Dr. O'Connor from Scotland. He'll be here soon. But Lace. The babies. They were early. You sure they're all right?" Damn but he needed to see them, hold them. Check them for all their toes and fingers. Look into their eyes. And Lacy. He wanted to kiss her and tell her to her face how amazing she was. Fuck.

"Ian has them in some kind of incubator for now. Just to be on the safe side. But they each weighed a little over four pounds. He was thrilled. If Ian is ever thrilled about anything. You know how he is. Anyway, he's been giving them a thorough going over and says they look perfect. Wants me to name one of them Ian. Says it's only right."

"Like hell. We settled on those names and I like them. You okay that they're all a little on the Latino side?"

"Yeah, I like it. They go with the last name. Of course Mama's not sold. Cats have their own ways of naming children. The names are important." Lacy cleared her throat. "We can wait until you get home to talk about middle names. We can use those to help with the cat side of the family. It'll be soon, won't it?"

"Not sure how soon." Rafe hated to say it. "I have to finish this, Lace. It may take a while. We're going after the poisoner. It's across the Atlantic. Can you deal with the delay?"

"If I have to. Don't worry about me. Take care of your family. I know how it is. I'm dealing with mine." She sighed. "Got to go, Ian's bringing me one of the babies. I think it's Gabriel. You should see him. Little legs kicking. Maybe he'll play soccer. Wouldn't that be cool? Anyway, I'm going to try nursing him. Sorry you can't see this."

"And that Ian can. Shit." Rafe realized she'd ended the call. Ian putting one of his sons

to Lacy's breast. The picture in his head made him crazy. He looked around at the sad little village and wanted to take a torch to it all. Why the hell was he stuck here in his past when his future was five thousand miles away?

CHAPTER SIX

"You have a sample of the poison?" Bart sniffed the bottle and held it up to the light. "I can do an analysis. See if I can figure out what it is. Maybe we'll get lucky and it's something I've run across before." He and Caitlin Campbell had just arrived. Cait knew enough about medicine, thanks to a background in med school, to help her lover. "Wait here and I'll let you know what I think after I examine your grandfather." Bart nodded.

Rafe paced the living room. Grandfather didn't believe in doctors, most shifters didn't, and Rafe could hear him letting them know it, loudly. A woman doctor? Even worse. Matias almost came unglued when he realized that the doctors were "blood suckers." He bellowed for his grandson, reminding him that in another hour these two would be dead and useless. Rafe had forgotten that inconvenient truth.

"Just let Dr. O'Connor see if he can help, *Abuelo*. You called me here. I trust this man. If he can save you, let him try." Rafe stared down at his frail grandfather who was just as stubborn as the day he'd left the clan, centuries ago. To his shock, the old man just nodded.

"Go. Step outside so you don't have to see my

humiliation, boy. I feel my spirit about to leave my body. What's the worst they can do? Hasten its departure?" He turned his head on the pillow and closed his eyes.

Rafe nodded, more depressed than he'd ever been, and left the room. An hour later the vampires came out.

"Okay, here's what we know." Bart looked serious as he wiped his hands on a towel. "Your grandfather must have been in excellent physical shape when he ingested the poison to have fought it off this long. It would have killed most men instantly, even a shape-shifter."

Caitlyn put her hand on Rafe's arm. "He's a fighter, isn't he?" She was trying to comfort him.

"He's going downhill, though. I've only been here a day and I've seen it." Rafe rubbed his burning eyes. He needed sleep but was damned if he could keep his eyes closed even when he tried.

"I'll get right on that sample." Bart didn't waste time denying the fact that Grandfather was dying. "Our best bet right now is to either find an antidote or make one. Matias said you're on the hunt for the poisoner. I'd be willing to bet he'll have an antidote handy. It's only wise when you're dealing with poisonous substances. In case of an accident." He glanced at the window where they could see the false dawn, a sure sign that the real one wasn't far away. "Sorry about the timing. Cait and I must rest. I'm sure that's maddening for you shifters."

"Yes, but we'll deal with it. I'm just grateful you studied medicine. Shifters rarely bother. We're usually a healthy race. Now I'm leaving with my people in an hour because I've got a lead on who did this. I'm trusting you with Grandfather's life. That's not a popular notion around here, putting faith in a vampire. But I have a history with your type and it's taught me that we do better in this world when we work together. Am I wrong?"

"No, you're exactly right. I'll do my level best to fight this poison and save your grandfather's life." The doctor looked solemn. "I wish I could promise you he'd pull through but there are no guarantees in medicine. How are your people going to react if Matias doesn't make it? I understand he's the leader of this clan. The shifter version of a laird if you were in Scotland. Do I need a quick exit strategy?" He gripped Caitlin's hand. "We won't be martyrs for this, you ken."

"I've made it clear you are to be treated well, no matter the outcome. My grandmother will back me on this and they'll listen to her, even if they won't listen to me." Rafe glanced at his grandfather's door, silently praying that this vampire would come up with a cure. "Grandmother's convinced it's a woman who did this. That's who I'm going after. She's the one who will be blamed if Matias dies, not you. The clan understands that you're our last resort. Do what you can, O'Connor, but no one here expects miracles." But he'd get down on his knees and thank God if one did happen.

The doctor nodded. "I've seen a few in my long life and I'll do my damnedest to give you one." He pulled a paper out of his pocket. "Here's a list of things I'll need to set up a proper lab. If I'm to work on an antidote, I need to get started immediately. So have this here by sunset."

Rafe glanced at the paper. His grandmother could handle the list and start proving that she really did want the old man to pull through. "You'll have it." He held out his hand. "Thanks for coming and you can be sure no one will disturb your death sleep. You have my word on it. I'll post a guard at your bedroom door." He didn't miss the glance the doctor and Cait exchanged. "Yes, I know it's a little late for reassurances."

"I'm here because Gloriana thinks the world of you. If Cait's brother's new wife trusts you, then so shall we. And a guard would be appreciated. Sleeping in a strange house is uncomfortable for us. I won't deny that." Bart flashed a grin. "And we left our double wide coffin at home."

Rafe slapped him on the shoulder. "Funny. I lived with Glory too many years to believe that. But I get that you're vulnerable during the day. I will ask my grandmother to pick her most trustworthy man to sit at your door. Not everyone here knows and likes vampires. I wouldn't risk either of you for the world."

Cait kissed Rafe's cheek. "Now I know why Glory counts you as her best friend. I admit I've been worrying about sunrise ever since we got here."

"Even Blade tolerates you. And your history with him isn't the best." Bart smiled and nodded. "I like those precautions and appreciate them. Now show us where we can sleep. I feel the dawn and would like a shower first."

Rafe left them to the housekeeper's care. He had a dozen details to iron out if he was to push off for the port in an hour. He had words with his grandmother first, making sure she knew just how serious he was about keeping the vampires safe. When he was positive that she got it, he checked on supplies. At least his volunteers were just as eager to find the poisoner and the antidote as he was and were working tirelessly to get ready to go.

Matias may have been weak when it came to women, but he still had the respect that being clan leader gave him. The Castillo name went a long way in this village. Unless it was tainted with demon blood. Rafe heard whispers and caught the villagers giving him sidelong glances as he tried to get everything organized.

He looked around the square. In some ways the place hadn't changed in centuries. Oh, yes, there was Wi-Fi and satellite TV now, but the stone buildings were the same and so were the people. He couldn't imagine Lacy or his children here, stuck in a time warp. But it had been a great place to grow up, surrounded by family. That is until he'd become a teenager and started coming into his powers. He'd thought it was funny to use his eyes as a flame thrower. His cousins hadn't gotten the joke. No one would come near him after that unless they thought they could use him in a prank. He'd always end up with the blame, even if another boy had pushed him into a situation. He had developed a big chip on his shoulder then that only his brothers ignored.

Matias and his grandmother had done their best to give him a happy home, but raising a demon child was probably doomed from the start. Rafe remembered loud fights with Grandfather when the older man had refused to accept that his grandson was no longer a child to be ordered to follow what he saw as arbitrary rules. That was undoubtedly typical when a boy became a man. Rafe would have to remember that when his own boys grew up. His boys. God. Such a responsibility. And then there was his daughter. How would he keep them safe?

Rafe was the first to admit that the modern world was a dangerous place. Did he really want to raise his children surrounded by mortals and other paranormals?

But bringing them here wasn't the answer. It had been over a thousand years since Rafe had lived here as a child. And he'd been loved here only because of his grandfather's strong personality and insistence that Rafe be treated as part of the clan. He'd had to fight for his place here and had finally lost that fight. His own children would be half were-cat as well. They'd never be accepted here. Neither would Lacy. And was this even a safe place now? Obviously not, since Grandfather lay dying just yards away.

Rafe kicked a loose stone out of his way and strode toward his grandfather's house again. He could count on one hand the people he'd recognized since he'd arrived here. The clan was in danger of extinction and unless something drastic happened, the Castillo name would soon be meaningless. Matias had to live and change his ways, become the man he'd once been, charismatic and worth following. If not, Grandmother needed to take the reins and become a stronger leader. The condition of the village made it clear she'd let many things slide even before Matias had become ill. Rafe needed to find her again and make sure she'd already put that guard on O'Connor's door. Then he was going to say a few words to her about the conditions here. She wasn't going to like it but, in his current mood, he really didn't give a damn.

"I feel fine. I have to get up and out of here." Lacy couldn't stand all the hovering another minute. Her mother wouldn't leave her alone for a minute. Apparently seeing a vampire doctor working over her daughter had made her mom lose all common sense. She'd gone from hysterical over the drug Ian had used to ease Lacy's pain to raving about how to feed the babies.

"Where did this formula come from?" Her mother grabbed the bottle Lacy was holding. "Put the baby to your breast. I told you it's healthier."

"There are three of them, Mama. I'm worn out trying to feed them myself. They eat like they're starving all the time. I can't possibly have enough milk for all of them." Lacy winced when the baby lying in her lap stared at her and screamed. "Now see what you've done. Give me the bottle. Ian says that's a high quality formula. I called him and he researched it. I had Amy go out and buy it. See? Lucas loves it."

Her mother stared at her, squinting and wrinkling her nose as if trying to read her mind. She couldn't of course. She did hand over the bottle and couldn't complain when the baby grabbed the nipple and began sucking hungrily.

"He does seem to like it. But, Lacy, you could do both. A little of you, a little of the bottle. And I will speak to Amy, your partner in crime. You shouldn't be keeping secrets from me." She frowned. "Suddenly putting them on formula. You're not thinking of leaving them, are you? It's only been a week since you gave birth. And there was that long labor." Mama picked up another one of the babies who'd started fussing. ""What's the matter, Daniela?" She bounced the baby in her arms until she settled down. "Tell me the truth now, Lacy. Are you thinking of going after that man?"

"That man is the father of these children." Lacy laid aside the empty bottle and put the baby on her shoulder to burp him. "I'm worried about Rafe. What if his grandfather dies? He'll need me. All I'm doing here is lying around like an invalid. You're taking care of the children anyway."

"I can fix that. I'll leave you alone with them. They're yours. *You* do everything. I thought I was doing you a favor. Giving you time to heal from a rough birth. But I can stop right now." Her mother stomped around the bed, finally putting Daniela in her crib. "You are not going after that man."

"I have to, Mama. I have a bad feeling. Maybe it's my raging hormones, I don't know. But I need to see Rafe, make sure he's all right." Lucas enjoyed a noisy burp then added a bit of formula to the blanket she'd put under his head. "Oops. Got a little mess here. Will you take him?"

"Hah! What if I say no?" But Sheila grabbed him anyway, cooing to him and wiping his chin before she kissed his head and tucked him into his own bassinet. "How could you leave these precious babies? Look at them, sleeping now. And I don't believe in your feelings. I know how cats are after they give birth. You are having the usual reaction. You will heal fast then get crazy with lust." She threw up her hands. "Go see your fancy vampire doctor. See what he says about you travelling in your condition. I bet he tells you to stay the hell home."

"I'll go see Ian, Mama. That's a good idea. But staying here and worrying isn't happening. I'm going after Rafe." Lacy sat up and the room swayed. No, she wasn't giving in to it. She only felt woozy because her mother had insisted she nurse all three babies and they'd drained her. No wonder she was weak and dizzy. Lacy put her feet on the floor and waited for everything to settle into place. When it finally did, she picked up her phone. After she hung up, she faced her mother.

"He's going to see me this afternoon. But prepare yourself. I'm going. And I know you'll take care of my children because who else should I leave them with?" Lacy had grown up learning manipulation from her mother. Now she pressed home the point. "I guess I could go on-line and hire someone from one of those nanny services. Of course I could get a stranger who could care less if Gabriel chokes on his formula or Daniela rolls over and falls off the bed. But I have three children so coming home to one would be pretty good, don't you think?"

"Stop it. I know what you're doing. And I won't hear another word!" Her mother put her hands over her ears.

"Fine. Don't listen. But this afternoon Ian's going to give me a final checkup and something to get rid of this." She pressed her hands to her swollen breasts. "I know he's going to tell me I'm okay to travel."

Sheila hissed. "No, it's unnatural. You must stay here and do your duty as a mother. Will you listen to a vampire instead of your own family?" Of course her mom would pull out that argument. She and Ian had bickered constantly while they'd been in his home.

"Ian is an excellent doctor. Look at the results. Three perfect children even though they were early." Lacy was ready to head to the shower but she needed to get some things settled first. "I'm going after Rafe. You can either watch the babies here or I'm taking them with me. An airplane ride for newborns might be a little rough, but I can handle it. Maybe Ian has a harmless drug he can give them so they'll sleep through it." She hid a grin when her mother gasped. "And I'm sure Rafe's relatives in the shifter clan would be thrilled to see the babies and take care of them."

"Drugs!" Her mother stood in front of the cribs like she dared Lacy to touch them. "I know you have to be kidding me. Of course they're too little to travel. I won't hear of it. I can take care of them." Mama looked down at the babies and muttered something about shifters. Then

GERRY BARTLETT

she turned and glared at Lacy. "You exhaust me."

"I'm sorry. But thanks, Mama."

"Where's your pride? Chasing halfway across the world after that shifter is not a good idea, Lacy. He'll either come home to his family or he won't. Wait and see." Clearly her mother hoped they'd seen the last of Rafe. Her own love life had taught her that men were superfluous. She'd raised Lacy and her siblings mostly on her own.

"No. I'm not waiting." Lacy was pleased that she was steady now and so was the room.

"Be careful when you see that vampire doctor. I don't like him. I swear, he wanted a taste of--"

"Mama, stop! Ian was pulling your chain. I saw him flash his fangs when you were around. But he'd never touch them to one of the babies." He'd actually laughed to Lacy about her mother's paranoia behind her back. "I need to be sure I'm healed before I go see Rafe." Lacy could feel herself flush. "I, I miss him."

"Hormones! Yes, go twitch your tail at your man." Her mother shook her head. "You're killing me, you know. There are so many nice cats who would love you, respect you. Men who come from good families. At least promise you won't marry him yet." Her mother actually got tears in her eyes.

"Will you quit disrespecting Rafe?" Lacy knew she couldn't afford to fight with Sheila now. She did need her to babysit, but this was getting old. "I love him and I'm going to marry him. He gave me these beautiful children. He will be in my life forever because of that no matter what happens after this." Her own eyes filled but she didn't let a tear fall. The certainty that Rafe needed her wouldn't go away. She had to go to him. And, fussing or not, her mother would guard her grandchildren with her life.

Mama put her arm around Lacy and stood beside her as they gazed down at the babies who slept the sleep of the innocent.

60

"You understand why this is so hard for me, Alençon?"

"Mama, please. You promised to never call me that." Her mother had named her after what she called the queen of lace, a favorite of hers. The name was an embarrassment that her daughter had insisted be forgotten as soon as she was old enough to have her name legally changed to Lacy.

"I am very serious now. You are the one who tied yourself to this shifter. They are not like us. He could decide to stay there. With his so-called clan." She brushed a hand over one child's head and sighed. "Would you leave us? To be with him? Take these little ones to a strange place? What if these babies turn out to be cats?"

Lacy pulled away from her mother. "This knee-jerk mistrust of other paranormals has to stop. Rafe is a fine man and a good provider. He owns his own successful business. If a were-cat with his kind of money and character had come to you asking to marry me, you would be over the moon right now."

"Hah! Did he come to me? Ever?" Mama had her hands on her hips, eyes flashing. "Hell no. He knocked you up." She put up her hand when Lacy started to say something. "Oh, let me finish. I know you had a lot to do with that. You were in heat, my girl. Panting after him. What man could resist?" She wagged a finger in Lacy's face. "I don't regret these children. What I regret is the blood that is now mixed with ours."

"Stop it!" Lacy jumped when all three babies woke with screams. "Now see what you've done. You keep spouting that venom and I'll make sure you never see these children grow up. Is that what you want? To alienate me and my family? I'll do it. I swear I will. I'll take them and go wherever Rafe wants to go." She picked up two at a time, gesturing to her sister, who had come running when the screaming started, to get the third. She began to croon, soothing them quickly. "We can sell his club and live anywhere. Think about that."

"You are so stubborn. You take after your father, that no account tom cat." Mama reached for Lucas, nestled in Amy's arms. "I will not say another word. I just remembered that my own taste in men is not worth spit." She kissed the baby's cheek. "At least we make beautiful children. So go to your man. I will guard these babies with my life as you knew I would." She laid him in his crib. "Precious boy. I believe someday you will be a fine strong cat like your grandma, won't you big fellow?"

"He might." Lacy relented and handed her Daniela after placing a kiss on her downy head.

"This beauty. She will break all the boys' hearts. Look at her. She has your red hair, Lacy."

"Unfortunately. I'm lucky Rafe likes it." Lacy took Gabriel from her sister. "I swear they all look like Rafe to me." She sighed and just breathed in his baby scent, tears stinging her eyes. She hated to leave them. But her instincts had never failed her yet. Rafe needed her and he would have her. "I'll be back and bring you your papa." She laid her son in his crib and gave her mother one more searching look.

"I said nothing. He is their father. I have never argued that point. Come back safely. We will plan a wedding."

"Good." Lacy began getting dressed. Amy drove her to Ian's where she got a clean bill of health and a lecture about the medication that would dry up her milk. Ian thought she should continue to breast feed too. As a supplement for the children. Amazing that he and her mother agreed on something. He reluctantly gave her the drug anyway after she insisted she was going to be leaving for a week, maybe longer.

Then she called Ed. They were going to an island off the coast of Spain. Imagine. She would finally get to see where Rafe came from. If she didn't have this sense that there was a dark cloud of danger, the kind that made the hairs on the back of her neck stand on end, surrounding him, she might have cancelled the trip and stayed home.

Leaving the babies was harder than she'd thought it would be. But she couldn't ignore the growing sense of urgency she felt that she needed to be with Rafe.

With a litany of her mother's complaints in her ears, Lacy made her arrangements. No one was stopping her until she saw for herself that Rafe was all right.

"Rafe belongs to Clan Castillo. That's Rafael's real last name. Not Valdez." Ed sighed, obviously giving up on getting comfortable. The big man wasn't built for a coach seat. Neither was Lacy but she simply couldn't afford two first class tickets to the Spanish Canary Islands, where Rafe's clan lived.

"Castillo. Are you freaking kidding me?" Lacy wanted to hit something. It said something about their relationship that she didn't even know Rafe's real last name. She should have figured out that he wasn't really a Valdez though. Glory had told her once that Jerry had paid for her bodyguards for decades, all of them called Valdez. Rafe was just the latest in a long line of shape-shifters who'd gone by that name.

"It's an ancient clan. But shrinking all the time." He frowned, his elbow knocking Lacy's off her armrest. She decided to give it to him.

"Why? Cats stick together. We feel safer that way. Aren't shifters the same way?" She smiled, thinking about how nice it was to know that her children were surrounded by family right now.

"Shifters feel restricted by the old ways. Modern technology has made it easier to adapt to our environment and get along with mortals. You have no idea what the clan laws are like. The leaders control the purse strings too. Financial freedom is just one of the reasons many of the younger generation have taken off. Like Rafe and I did. My clan is Montenegro, based in Tunis, but my mother was a Castillo. So I feel loyalty to both clans and spent time with

Rafe's grandparents when I was young." Ed sighed and tried to lean his seat back. The woman behind him yelled and he stopped it halfway. "You'll see for yourself. Castillo clan headquarters is pretty much in the middle of nowhere on the island. But just a few miles away, in Santa Cruz, there's a resort that has the latest of everything and luxurious accommodations. Why be stuck in an archaic system when you can see what's possible if you have money of your own?"

"And Rafe's grandfather is head of his clan. Why won't he change things? He sent a private jet for Rafe so there's obviously money there." Lacy waved down the flight attendant. "Could I have a soda please?"

"Sure. Sir, anything for you?" The woman looked down at his long legs which he'd stretched into the aisle.

"Thanks. Diet for me." He smiled at the attendant but didn't answer until she moved on. "Matias is rolling in it. He sold a lot of property to developers when Santa Cruz became a resort decades ago. He still gets rents like you wouldn't believe and owns a few hot properties outright." Ed yawned. "But he's stubborn when it comes to the clan and he likes the old ways. That means he's the dictator and no one questions his authority."

"I can see how that wouldn't go over well with someone like Rafe. He's pretty strong willed himself." Lacy took her soda gratefully. "Thanks."

Ed nodded. "Exactly. So he left. A long time ago." He glanced at the woman on the other side of Lacy but she was asleep. "Did you happen to let him know we were coming?"

"Um, no. I was pretty sure he'd have told me to stay home." Lacy drained her soda. The caffeine was just what she needed but she still felt exhausted. They had hours yet to go but at least they'd lucked into a nonstop flight directly to Santa Cruz after they'd left Austin and landed in Houston where there were more international connections.

"I'd have told you the same thing, if my girl had just

gone through childbirth." Ed stared at her until Lacy looked away. "This is nuts, Lacy. What are you going to do when you get there? You could be a distraction for Rafe. When all is said and done, this is clan business." Ed drained his drink and pulled down his tray table, bumping his knees. "The family won't welcome your interference. Even if you are the mother of Rafe's children."

"Oh, yeah, I'm the mother of his children all right." Lacy looked down to where her blouse was showing signs of boob leakage. Damn it all. Ian's prescription to make her milk stop flowing had been designed for mortals. He had no idea if it worked on paranormals since this was a new situation for him. Lacy was very afraid that it wasn't doing the job if her aching breasts were any indication. She'd already made one trip to the bathroom and stuffed toilet paper in her bra.

"You know, Ed, I appreciate your take on the situation, thanks a lot. But I'm going over there for Rafe, not the freaking clan. If they don't like it, they can stuff it." Lacy set her glass next to his, aware that she was being pissy but she didn't care. "You shifters don't think much of cats, do you?"

"You're limited. You have one play. We can be anything." Ed talked quietly but still looked around to make sure no one was listening to them. "Even you have to admit there's only so much a cat can do."

"You haven't seen my cat, Ed. So keep your judgement to yourself. My play is pretty damned good, if I do say so myself. I'm not useless and I won't get in the way." This paranormal prejudice was getting on her last nerve. "Now I'm tired. Let me know when we're about to land." Lacy closed her eyes. She needed to rest. She hoped like hell her cat was up to some serious ass kicking. Cranking out three babies had taken more energy that she'd expected. Still, she would do whatever it took to help Rafe. Just let those shifters try to shut her out. She'd show them this kitty had claws.

CHAPTER SEVEN

By the time she and Ed got to the run down village in their rented car, Lacy knew she'd made a mistake. She had no energy, her body hurt, and even her breasts ached because that medication clearly wasn't working. Her blouse was soaked and she felt disgustingly dirty. When Ed stopped the rented Jeep in the middle of the village square, Lacy groaned.

"This is it? I'd say the Castillo Clan is in trouble. You're right. Compared to Santa Cruz, this is pitiful." She saw a child standing in a doorway. The little girl stared at them then ran to the large stone house at one end of the square.

"It is. Usually it looks better than this though." Ed frowned. "Matias started neglecting his duties as leader long before he got sick. Normally his wife would have picked up the reins before things got this bad but something's going on there. Obviously nothing's been done to fix up this place for some time." Ed climbed out of the car. "You look a little worse for wear. I knew you shouldn't have travelled so soon after having the babies."

"No lectures, please." Lacy got out of the car and pulled a sweater around her. She breathed in the cool, fresh air. Climate-wise this was a nice place. Then an elegant little woman dressed in black was walking toward her beside the child. Was the black for a funeral? Had Rafe's grandfather died?

"I am Iliana, temporary leader of the Clan Castillo." She smiled at Ed. "Eduardo, good to see you. Who have you brought with you?"

"This is Lacy Devereau, Rafael's intended, *Abuela*." Ed pulled Lacy forward. "She was determined to come. To see if she could help him or give him comfort. Is Grandfather ..."

"Matias is still with us. Not good, but not dead yet." Her mouth twisted and she patted his broad shoulder. Her eyes went to Lacy's stomach. "Rafael's woman. But, child, you were pregnant!"

Lacy put her hands over her stomach that was still too puffy to suit her. "I'm sure Rafe told you I had the babies days ago." Lacy pulled out her phone and showed the woman a picture. "Two boys and a girl. Aren't they beautiful? Daniela, Gabriel and Lucas."

"Yes. Beautiful. Those are good names for them. Strong. The boys are very like their father." She studied Lacy. "And Daniela favors you, of course." The woman gazed at the picture for a long moment. "Obviously cats give birth easily since you felt well enough to travel so soon. But still, you must be exhausted. Come inside and sit. Call me Iliana. And I will call you Lacy. An interesting name." Her dark eyes swept over Lacy again. "Rafael was always unpredictable. A were-cat. We will see what the children turn out to be. At what age does the cat appear in your family?" She turned and led the way to the big stone house.

"Puberty, Iliana. These babies may prove to be some of me, some of Rafe. There's no way to know until then. Unless your kind manifests earlier." Lacy really didn't have it in her to start a fight over this now. Rafe's grandmother hadn't exactly attacked her, but she hadn't been all warmth and hugs either. Lacy stumbled. Exhaustion washed over her and she realized she was about to fall to the ground. "Sorry. I hadn't realized..." She couldn't seem to form another sentence.

"Child! You are dead on your feet. Eduardo, pick her up." Iliana frowned at him. "You should never have let her travel. Even a cat has her limits."

"*Abuela*, you should understand that I cannot tell a woman what to do if she is determined." Ed picked up Lacy and carried her inside the house. He set her gently on a long sofa. "That was easier than the last time I toted you around, Lacy. Without the babies, you are light as a feather."

"Doubt it." Lacy took a bottle of water from Iliana gratefully and drank until she felt rational again. "Thank you. Is Rafe here?"

"No, I'm afraid you missed him. He is on his way to Morocco. He's trying to track down the *puta* who poisoned Matias." Iliana sat across from Lacy. "You look ill. We have a doctor here. As soon as the sun sets, I will ask him to look at you." She leaned close, as if to share a secret, and frowned. "I apologize but he is a vampire. I hope you can stand to have him help you."

"A vampire doctor?" Lacy fiddled with her soaked blouse. "Of course. My best friend is a vampire. And I could ask..." she looked at Ed and felt her cheeks warm. "Well, I took something to make my milk go away but it didn't work."

Iliana had straightened at the news that Lacy had vampires for friends. "Well! Of course you must know all kinds of people in America. I never saw the need to go there myself, but Rafael and Eduardo seem to find it fascinating." She stood and glanced at Ed, who stared down at his shoes.

"As for your breasts, no worries, *niña*. I have a remedy for that. There are herbs we've used for centuries. Wait here." Iliana left the room. She returned quickly and another woman hurried out the door into the square.

"Maria will find what you need and bring it to you. It will not harm you."

"Thank you. As soon as I take it, I want to go after Rafe." Lacy leaned back, trying to pull herself together. It was ridiculous to feel so tired. All she'd done was sit on planes for twelve hours.

"Why don't you lie down on the couch? I can't think you should go after Rafael. He has a small army with him. There will probably be a fight. Would he really want the mother of his children to be in danger now? With the babies so young?" Iliana practically shoved Lacy back against a cushion and pulled off her shoes so she could lift her feet onto the couch. For a little lady, she was strong.

"I'm going after him." Lacy didn't lift her head though. It felt too good to be stretched out like this. "A fight? I can fight at his side."

"I know cats. The only way to get to him is across the water. The Atlantic Ocean." Iliana smiled. "How do you feel about riding in a small boat to catch him? The waves hitting the keel, the salt spray in your face?" She looked like she wanted to laugh.

Lacy wanted to scratch her eyes out. Of course she hated water, all cats did. Salt spray in her face? Pure torture. But to be with Rafe again, she'd endure it. She pushed herself up on her elbows, struggling to sit.

"Maybe we'd better go now, Ed. I can rent a boat in the port where we landed to take me to Rafe. If you will give me some directions ..." Lacy shivered, the wet blouse getting to her, not to mention the pain in her breasts.

"Calm yourself, child. Here comes Maria. Drink this and relax until it takes effect. Then I will send a man with you to take you to Rafael if you insist. We have a small boat with a driver who will know where to go. He can catch up to the yacht that the men and women have taken to Morocco. It is just a few hours away if you are in a hurry." Iliana sniffed the dark liquid in the glass and nodded. "Perfect. Drink up. This will do the trick."

"You are sure?" Lacy smelled it herself. Not bad. She sipped. Oh, why not? No way was she seeing Rafe leaking like a dairy cow overdue for its milking. Not sexy. Weres healed very fast and Ian had assured her she was ready for sex if Rafe still wanted her. Too bad she looked like she still had a baby inside her. Damned swollen stomach. Why hadn't it snapped back in place? She'd been horrified when she'd seen the lumpy mass she'd been left with after childbirth. In the week since it had smoothed out some but it was still bigger than she liked.

Didn't matter. She wanted *him* and couldn't wait to be in his arms again. It had been too long since she'd seen Rafe. She downed the drink, set the empty glass on the coffee table, and fell back on the couch again.

"That's right. Rest. Eduardo, come with me. I want to hear about this Austin, Texas, where you and my Rafael have been living. What is so wonderful about it? I hear he has a dance club there." Iliana dragged Ed to the other side of the room. Lacy rested her hands on her chest, waiting for relief. What had been in that potion anyway? Her eyelids were growing heavy. Even though she tried to stay awake and hear what Ed was telling his grandmother, before she knew it she fell asleep.

"Did you drug me?" Lacy sat up and yawned. It was dark outside now and she recognized the man standing next to Rafe's grandmother. The Scottish vampire doctor. He'd been at Glory's wedding.

"Just a little something to help you relax." Iliana nodded. "Doctor O'Connor is ready to help you. Would you like me to leave you alone with him?"

"Yes." Lacy didn't have much to say to the lady. Obviously she didn't want Lacy going after Rafe. Well, it was none of her damned business what Lacy did.

"How do you feel?" Dr. O'Connor sat on the coffee table in front of Lacy and looked her in the eyes.

"Like I need a hot shower. Can you believe that

woman? She gave me something that was supposed to get rid of my milk but wiped me out instead."

"It might have done both. You want to check or shall I?" He glanced at her blouse. The milk had dried into a stiff mess.

"Go ahead. I'm used to vampire doctors. Ian MacDonald delivered my babies."

"So I heard. He called me bragging about it." Dr. O'Connor carefully unbuttoned her top and examined her. "Well, whatever was in Iliana's potion did the trick. Your swelling is down and you aren't leaking fluid. Good job, I'd say. How do you feel otherwise?"

"I'm healed. Shifters do quickly, you know. Ian can vouch for that. He examined me right before I left town." Lacy sat up and pulled her top together. She was desperate to get out of her filthy clothes.

"All right then. I have another patient who needs me so I'll leave you to shower and change. Then Iliana says you can find her and a gentleman named Ed in the courtyard." He turned. "Here's Caitlin to show you where you can get cleaned up."

"Blade's sister!" Lacy smiled at the woman who came down the stairs. "Fancy meeting you here."

"Strange, isn't it? I hope my brother and Glory are enjoying their honeymoon. He wouldn't tell anyone where they were going. Not even Glory." Cait smiled. "Come with me and I'll fix you up. Your luggage is in a bedroom with adjoining bath. I heard you had quite a greeting here."

"I doubt Rafe's grandmother is excited to have a were-cat join the family but she'll have to get over it." Lacy followed Cait up the stairs. "When he hears she drugged me, he's not going to be happy."

"I wouldn't tell him if I were you." Cait stopped in front of a door. "Let her play her little tricks. In the end, you've had his children and will have his heart."

"Yes, he even proposed but I was stupid enough to balk. You know he and Glory had a history . . ." Lacy felt even surer now since she'd been away from Rafe that she'd been crazy to hesitate when he'd asked her. It felt like forever since he'd held her in his arms. She realized Cait was staring at her. "Well, I'm over my insecurities. When I find him I'm getting the ring from Rafe, putting it on my finger and never taking it off."

"Good." Cait hugged her. "Don't make a big deal out of Grandmama's snit. When you live forever, you can't afford to feud with the family."

"Excellent point. Now can you tell me how Rafe's grandfather is doing? I know Dr. O'Connor is here for him." Lacy leaned against the bedroom door.

Cait frowned. "I'm afraid Matias isn't going to make it. Rafe has gone after an antidote for the poison but time is critical. Bart's working on making one of his own, but that takes time and he's had no luck yet."

"Oh, wow. I'm sorry to hear that." Lacy knew whoever had poisoned the man wasn't just going to hand the antidote over to Rafe either. "Well, I'm glad you two are here trying to save him anyway. Thanks." She finally headed into the bedroom where her suitcase had been put on the bed. She pulled out fresh clothes and undressed quickly. A hot shower did wonders for her attitude. She was going after Rafe, ready to help if he needed her.

Of course there was that ocean to cross first. The Atlantic. The glimpse she'd gotten out of the plane window had made it look vast and forbidding. Oh, well, cats didn't like water but they could handle anything if they had to. By the time she was walking across the courtyard toward Rafe's grandmother, Lacy had managed to convince herself that she could control her temper. She would show Iliana that Rafe had made a smart choice when he'd picked this cat for his mate.

"Iliana, thanks so much for the refreshing sleep. It was just what I needed. The doctor agreed that I'm in fighting form and your potion worked perfectly." Lacy crossed her fingers behind her back. Not exactly what the doctor had said but she was entitled to exaggerate a bit after being drugged against her will. "Ed, are you with me on this trip across the sea?" Lacy wanted to laugh at the look on Iliana's face. Oh, so worth it.

"Sure. I've found out there's a speedboat and driver in the harbor we can use and I've got the details now on where they were headed." Ed exchanged looks with Iliana. "Of course if luck is with them, they've already handled it and are on their way home now. We may be wasting our time."

"He is right. Are you sure you should go? Lacy, your children need you. It is foolish to take chances. Rafael and the others can handle this. You can wait for him here." Rafe's grandmother twisted her fingers together.

"I want to be there to help, Iliana. Surely you understand that. You seem to be a strong woman yourself." Lacy smiled at Ed. "Are we ready now?"

"Do as you wish but be careful. This is rainy season. Storms can pop up at any time." Iliana's smile was strained.

"I'm sure we'll be fine." But Lacy glanced up at the sky as she climbed into the jeep. Just what she needed, worry about the damned weather. "I hope Grandfather hangs in there." And with that she snapped her seatbelt and waited for Ed to start the car. Rafe. She'd go through a hurricane if she had to if that's what it took to be in his arms again and to feel the magic between them. It had been too long.

CHAPTER EIGHT

"They've seen the yacht and recognized it." Tomas had shifted into bird form and scouted the enclave of the Moroccan clan. "The woman who had the affair with Grandfather is there all right. Shiloh. Seems the clan members suspect we're after her. There's even some discussion about whether to turn her over to us or not. But she runs the show so that talk's going nowhere. Anyone who turned traitor in her clan wouldn't last long there."

"Did they know for sure that she poisoned Matias or is it just a rumor?" Rafe paced the deck. Miguel was captaining the ship which was fine with him. He'd never been into sailing and didn't know much about navigation either. The voyage had been ridiculously long though. A trip that should have taken a few hours had taken days. There'd been one disaster after another—engine trouble that had resisted repairs, then storms, steering problems and even a flock of kamikaze seagulls that had done something to the GPS and forced them off course and cost them hours. Now they were finally near the area where Shiloh reigned supreme. Miguel was convinced the voyage was cursed. It had almost seemed like it.

"Has Shiloh admitted to poisoning Matias?" Tomas spit over the side of the ship. "She doesn't bother to deny it. She's used poison before when she wanted to get rid of someone. I heard two men talking about it."

"Any ideas about how to take her without a fight?" Rafe knew he needed a plan.

"I say we shift and go in when they're asleep. We can take her from her bed and make her talk." Marguerite was obviously eager to supervise the "make her talk" part of that.

"What's to keep her from waking the rest of them?" Tomas shook his head. "We need to be clever. Clearly we can't overpower them. I figure they outnumber us three to one. I didn't see that many men but there are plenty of houses. It's hot enough that many could be staying inside until it cools off after dark."

Rafe had heard enough. "I'm going to shift so I can see this place for myself. They might decide to take action and attack us, if they think we're after Shiloh. Stay alert."

"Someone has already flown over here and checked to see if Matias was on deck. They were buzzing about how you and I were here but not the old man. Big speculation about who would lead the clan if Matias was gone." Tomas grimaced. "I had an idea that I would be the one to--"

"You should be, brother. Or *Abuela*. I don't want it. You can rest easy on that score. But we'll deal with that later." Rafe squeezed his brother's shoulder. "I'm still going to go take a look." He shifted and flew up and over the land until he came to a large cluster of white-washed buildings surrounded by a stone fence. It was essentially a fortress. Men and women were occupied doing various tasks in a central courtyard. There were mechanics working on a couple of trucks, some women gossiping while they took down dry laundry and a few children playing soccer. A half a dozen men were seated at a table drinking, with rifles near at hand. There was no way his group wouldn't be outnumbered if it came down to a battle. He flew back to the ship, thinking hard.

"Any ideas, brother?" Tomas looked to him for answers, just like he had when they were kids.

"What if I go in and ask to meet her? Tell her I am Matias's heir and that I want to thank her if she did poison him. That I'd given up ever inheriting his fortune and the clan. I'd heard how beautiful she was and wanted to see for myself the woman who'd managed to bring my grandfather down. I'm sure it's common knowledge that Matias and I didn't get along. She should buy that." Rafe nodded at his brother. "I doubt people here would know he actually sent for me. What do you think?"

"I think gossip travels on the wind. They know that I had Lucia's beans for breakfast before I can pass a good fart." Tomas got a laugh for that one.

"What if I go to Shiloh right now?" Rafe saw the laughter die around him. "What have I got to lose?"

"Your life, man." Miguel turned the ship's wheel over to his first mate. "I know her. Who do you think brought Matias over here when he was involved with her? They used this yacht like their own personal love boat." He shook his head. "It sickened me to see my clan leader in such a state. A lovesick man led around by his *pene*. The woman is a witch, I tell you, to make Matias lose his mind that way."

"That doesn't sound like Grandfather. He always had his women, but stayed in control of his relationships." Rafe didn't like what he was hearing.

"Not this time. She is a beauty but with a heart of stone, Rafael. Be careful. If you think you can fool her, you are wrong. This is no ordinary woman. There is more going on here than a woman with wiles. She has powers and Matias was under her spell."

"Come now. Are you seriously claiming she used witchcraft on him?" Rafe started to laugh but the solemn faces around him stopped him cold. "You're serious."

"Damned right. So tell me, Rafael. What is this plan?

Are you going to try to convince her that you want her to be *your* mistress now? You are handsome enough for her I suppose. And if she thinks you now run the clan that will interest her too. But you will have to play the part convincingly." Miguel raised a bushy eyebrow. "*Señor*, I mean *really* convincingly. And you a new father with a good woman waiting for you. I hope you aren't going to be the same kind of man as Matias. I gave him respect out of clan loyalty. He was our leader, but he had the morals of a wild dog."

"You have just insulted dogs everywhere, Miguel." Marguerite punched his arm. "But he is right, Rafael. I hate to think of you anywhere near that woman. I ran into Matias with her in Barcelona once. When she looked at me I felt soiled, like el Diablo himself had touched me. Yes, *mi amigo* is right. She is a *bruja* and a *puta*."

"But you really think she is the one who poisoned my grandfather? Why? If they were lovers. . ?"

"First, she made no secret of the fact that she wanted our clan for her own. She craves power. She already rules this clan but it is not enough for her." Miguel swept his arm toward that gleaming white fortress. "Second, Matias found his *escroto* and finally told her no when she demanded to take your grandmother's place."

"Seems she'd take out Grandmother then instead of Matias." Rafe shuddered at the thought.

"You think she didn't try?" Marguerite looked around at the cluster of shifters on the deck. "Oh, you people are so naïve. Of course Shiloh went after Iliana. But that woman, our real leader, is too smart for her. She will never be fooled by such as that scheming *putana*. There were some near misses. But Iliana will not drink anything she is not sure of nor eat from a plate she does not fix with her own hands. And she surrounds herself with loyal people. Shiloh could not bribe anyone to do her bidding, though she tried."

"You mean she actually asked a clansman to take out

my grandmother?" Rafe had already been anxious to get to Shiloh but this just made him more determined.

"Believe it, Rafael. Finally, in a fit of rage, Shiloh must have decided to punish Matias for resisting her. That's when she used the poison. It's the bitch's way." Marguerite glanced at Miguel.

"Yes. Here's how it happened. They met on this boat and dined together one last time. Had a huge fight and then she flew away. Matias sickened that night. After he drank the wine she'd left on the table." Miguel sighed deeply. "Matias even said that he knew she'd finally gotten the best of him. That's why we don't doubt she did it, Rafael. We must make her pay."

"*Sí!* Kill the bitch!" "*Vamos!*" "What are we waiting for?" The crowd was stirred up, muttering and coming closer.

Marguerite obviously was ready to see this done. "Matias is dying while we stand here and talk about it. What are we going to do? Hey? Can you get to her, Rafael? Find an antidote? Or do we try to take the fortress?"

Rafe didn't want to imagine being convincing with a witch who would poison her own lover. Cold? Heartless. Could he pretend to want her? He hoped to God it wouldn't come to that. He only had to either capture the woman or kill her and get the antidote. He wouldn't hesitate to take her out if he was sure of her guilt.

"I'm going in alone. I'll do my damnedest to get the antidote. Like you say, we have no time to waste." He looked around and saw nods of support and approval.

"We will have your back. Never doubt it. She is known for her potions. She can cure or kill. Ask any shifter in the area. Be clever and the antidote will be yours. I'm sure she thinks Matias is long dead. Play it that way." Miguel went back to take the ship's wheel. "I'm going to hide this boat in a cove not far from here. It's where we always docked. You can shift to her place from there. How far you go with her is up to you. Just be careful, *amigo*."

Rafe held onto the railing as the boat cut through the chop when they skirted the coastline. He'd wasted too much time getting here. He felt like he was jumping out of his skin. Time *was* running out for his grandfather. At least it was getting dark and the vampires must be awake now. Dr. O'Connor might have luck replicating the poison and coming up with his own antidote. But would he be too late? Rafe knew he couldn't count on a miracle from the doctor. He decided to take one more look at the settlement and gestured to his brother. They shifted and headed inland.

By the time two small brown birds sat on a wire above the shifter headquarters, he had almost talked himself into trying force. The men he'd seen earlier were still drinking and it would be easy to overpower them. The trucks were gone and so were the men who'd been working on them so that made the odds better too. But then he saw the woman who must be Shiloh. She walked around the central courtyard of the settlement as if she owned it, issuing orders that were quickly obeyed. Oh, yes, she was in charge here.

He'd lost sympathy for his grandfather and his infidelities a long time ago. But this woman . . . No wonder Matias had fallen under her spell. Her beauty took his breath. And the way she moved... It was as if she had invented sex and wanted to teach a man the secret of a satisfaction that he could only dream about. Rafe shook his head, and then ruffled his feathers.

He had to get a grip. She was just a female, prettier than many but not worth losing a life or family over. Then she looked up as if she could see him--not the bird, but the man. Her eyes gleamed with mischief and a knowledge that made him duck his head, hoping he was imagining that she might know his secret. When he looked up again she was still staring. She licked her lips, the flick of her tongue making his entire body heat and harden. How the hell did she do that? He wasn't going to sit here and watch her play the seductress. No way in hell. With a shriek he flew up and away, aware of his brother by his side.

"Jeez, did you feel that?" Tomas rubbed his hands over his face after they landed on the boat deck and shifted back. "That woman is dangerous."

"You felt it too?" Rafe bent over, breathing hard. "It's true then. She *is* a witch. That's the only thing that explains it. The power. Hell, it was crazy to feel it from so far away."

"I don't think you should approach her, bro. She will eat you for breakfast, lunch and dinner and use your bones for toothpicks." Tomas wasn't smiling. "Unless . . ." He looked down at the deck.

"What? Spit it out, *hermano*." Rafe put his hand on his brother's shoulder. "I need any ideas you've got. Did you see the trucks pull in while we were sitting there? I'd hoped they'd left and was thinking about attacking. But they'd obviously just gone out for supplies and more men. You know she's got to have the antidote. Plus, she has to pay. For what she did to Grandfather."

"This idea I have... You won't like it." Tomas shook his head. "Forget it, Rafael. Maybe your doctor can cure *Abuelo*. That woman scared me and I was a fucking bird, *hermano*."

Rafe wanted to shake his brother. "We didn't come this far to turn tail and run. Give. What's your idea?"

Tomas swallowed. "You remember, when we were kids. I've never forgotten the time Luis taunted you and you showed him what you could do. When you get really mad."

Rafe pulled his arm back to his side. "When I let out my demon, you mean." Shit. Of course his brother had never forgotten that. He'd fought for control of that part of himself his entire life. Certainly Lacy had never seen it. The shame of being half demon was one reason he'd left the clan in the first place. Seeing his own brothers terrified of him had sealed the deal in his decision to make his own way someplace else, where no one knew him.

"Dude, don't tighten up on me. It's a skill, valuable if you want to know the truth. I hope you've learned to use it to defend yourself when you need to. It'll scare the shit out of most people." Tom actually punched his arm, forcing a grin. "Sure scared me back then."

"Dude? Where have you been hanging out, Tomas? Not in the clan." Rafe was desperate to change the subject.

"Who would want to stay there? It's like everyone is just waiting for the end times, you know?" Tomas was back to staring at the deck. "Grandfather doesn't care about the clan anymore. He was all about this woman. *Abuela* was so pissed she just let the place go. You saw it. Most of our generation has left. What do I want to stay for? Yeah, I have family there but I've been scouting out other options. If we don't get dynamic leadership soon, I'm gone and my family with me." He finally glanced at his brother. "I mean it, bro. Things will have to change. When we have time maybe you can tell me about America. This place where you live. It's something I might consider."

"I get it." Rafe looked out at the water. "America. Austin, Texas. It's a great place. I've made a nice life there for myself. I have friends, a good business. I can help you get set up if you want to come."

"Yeah. When this is behind us." Tomas stood next to him and bumped his shoulder. "Don't do it, man. That bitch could get you killed."

"I owe Grandfather a lot. Maybe this." Rafe rubbed the back of his neck. "Speaking of people who owe Grandfather, where are Stephan and Paulo? Why aren't they here trying to help?" His other two brothers.

"Yeah, well, they left the clan not long after you did. Matias didn't want to try to track them down. He was bitter about them leaving. And they didn't have special skills like you have." Tomas looked away. "Shit, I guess Grandfather kind of expected you to go demon on Shiloh's sexy ass."

81

"Great, just great. No wonder you came after me with guns and a half a dozen soldiers." He laughed but knew it was a bitter sound. "Hey, at least you stayed the course here, brother. You really should be made clan leader if Matias doesn't make it." Rafe laid his hand on Tomas's shoulder.

"My wife says I'm not ambitious enough. She's been eager to leave for a century or more. But it's our clan, our name." Tomas leaned against the railing. "I think that means something, you know? But Grandmother doesn't think I have the *cojones* to be leader. Nothing I do can convince her otherwise. So I'll get the hell out before I'll stay and see her take over."

"I'm sorry." Rafe had a new respect for his brother. He wished he had time to sit and talk with him. About the future. Make plans. Instead he had to think about becoming demon. Something he'd avoided for more years than he could count. The very idea strung him tight. A swim would help calm him, level him out. He thought about stripping off and diving off the side of the boat but he didn't have time. His demon. Yeah, he could pull it out. But there was always the chance that he wouldn't be able to shove it back inside once he was done with it. No wonder his head pounded.

"I'm sorry if bringing up the demon thing upsets you, bro. Seriously, I have no idea how you deal with it." Tomas cleared his throat. "I don't give a shit that you're part demon. I love you, *hermano*."

"Back at you. And thank you." Rafe hugged it out with Tom. Then he was back at the rail, struggling with the decision he knew he had to make. "But upset? That's like calling a tsunami a wavelet. I hate that part of me, Tomas. If I could cut it out, I would." They were alone, the rest of the group down below. Rafe could hear them arguing about strategy. A waste of time. This was all on him now and he knew it. "But it's there and, you're right, I might as well use it. Shiloh has power that an ordinary shifter couldn't hope to win against."

"Sorry. If there were another way…" Tom turned away from the shoreline, looking out to sea. "Do you hear what I hear?"

"Speedboat. Coming fast." Rafe squinted in the same direction. "Head below and tell the crew to arm themselves and come up ready to defend the boat."

"Right." Tomas was off on a run.

Rafe watched the small boat coming toward them in the gloom of dusk. There were three people on board. Not a real threat unless…

"Well, shit. What is she thinking?" Because he'd know that wild mane of red hair anywhere. His heart jumped in his chest and he wanted to fly to meet her. Kiss her until she was breathless, then shake some sense into her. How was he going to deal with this other woman when Lacy was here? And seeing her bright eyes shining across the water, he knew she'd never let him go into battle alone. His woman. Brave, beautiful and headstrong. The night had just gotten crazier. What man wanted to tangle with a wet cat?

CHAPTER NINE

"What the hell are you doing here, Lace?" Rafe helped her up the ladder they'd lowered over the side.

"Nice greeting, lover." Lacy ignored his frown and kissed him until he jerked her close, knocking the breath from her. His mouth opened over hers hungrily until he finally gentled the kiss then pulled back. Lacy wasn't about to let go. She inhaled his masculine scent that she knew as well as her own. God, she'd missed him.

"Look at you, you're soaked. What were you doing in an open boat like that? Where's your life jacket?" Rafe brushed her wet hair away from her flushed face. He leaned over the railing and said something harsh to the driver she and Ed had hired to bring them here. A rapid fire exchange in Spanish ended with Rafe tightening his grip on her. "You're lucky you didn't get tossed overboard. Careless bastard."

"Yeah, well, we did tell him it was an emergency. Paco, that's his name, took us seriously. He drove like he was making one of those James Bond movies." Lacy glanced at Ed, who'd come on board behind her. "We flew across the water. I should have put on a life vest though." She heard the man in the speedboat shout one last thing to Rafe before he reversed then headed out. God, she'd never been so scared in her life. The sea had been endless. The swells in the freaking Atlantic Ocean were enormous and no one had mentioned a life jacket. The boat had bumped over swells like it was *trying* to toss her overboard. She'd clung to the railing for dear life. Ed had looked like he was in his element, laughing as the spray hit their faces.

"Where is Paco going?" A burly man wearing a captain's hat walked up next to Rafe.

"He said he's going up the coast a ways to a safe harbor with some facilities. He needs to refuel and he'll probably tie up there. He was pretty sure we're in for a storm tonight." Lacy shivered. Looking up at the gathering clouds didn't reassure her. "He's a cowardly son of a bitch. We tried to get him to leave last night but he wouldn't take off until after sunrise."

"Sounds like Paco. I know the place." The captain shrugged. "But he's right about the weather." He slapped the steel railing. "Something to think about, Rafael. If you're planning to move on Shiloh soon. We've got a couple of hours maybe before the sky opens up, I'm thinking." He nodded toward the part of the boat that housed the ship's wheel. "I'll be checking the weather. Let me know what you decide but, for now, I think you have your hands full." He smiled at Lacy. *"¿Es verdad?"*

"You're right." Rafe made the introductions then looked down to where Lacy's claws had come out and were digging into his sides. "Lacy, sweetheart. You need to get out of those wet clothes. Obviously that was a rough trip."

"Yeah. Cats and water. Not our favorite thing. You're right. I'd kill for dry clothes. Too bad I left my suitcase sitting in your grandfather's house. I had a few words with your grandmother and made a grand exit. That cost me. I wouldn't go back for it because of my stupid pride." Lacy shivered, aware of the dozen or so people crowding the deck who were eyeing her. Some looked friendly, some curious and some definitely hostile. A glance at Rafe showed he wasn't smiling either.

"She give you a hard time?" Rafe kept his arm around her. "How is Grandfather?"

"He's still alive, thank God. But Iliana didn't think I should bother you. Since you were on a mission to get the antidote. Have you gotten it yet?" Lacy held her breath, hoping he'd done it and they were getting ready to just go back to Santa Cruz.

"No, I'm planning to try to take it soon." He now looked downright grim.

"Oh, Rafe. Tell me what I can do to help." Lacy clung to his side, getting him wet, but she couldn't seem to care.

"You can get into some dry clothes first." He looked around and gestured.

A smiling woman stepped out of the crowd. "Come with me, *carina*. I'm Chica. I'm sure I can find you something dry to wear." She winked at Rafe. "So this is your woman, Rafael. Chasing you across the world right after giving you three babies. Not bad, *primo*."

"Chica, Lacy. If you can help her out, I'd appreciate it." Rafe nodded. "I have plans to make."

"Thanks, Chica." Lacy stopped when the little blond started to lead her toward some stairs. "Rafe?" He kept staring at her. "Are you sorry I followed you here?"

He pulled her to him again for another kiss. "I missed you like hell. Any other time I'd be glad to see you. But your timing isn't great. There's going to be some serious shit going down here soon. You could be in danger." He shook his head. "Where are the babies? Are they okay? And you? Baby, you just gave birth. I hope you didn't travel too soon."

He looked her over from her wet head to her bare feet. Of course her shoes were in that speedboat that was no longer even a speck on the horizon. Where was her head these days? At least Rafe didn't seem to care that she looked horrible, he just seemed worried. Okay, she could deal with that. Lacy held up one hand.

"First, I'm fine, checked out by doctors and everything. The babies are thriving and my mother is doing her best to make sure they are fed, diapered and pampered to within an inch of their little lives." She ran a fingertip over Rafe's jaw, his five o'clock shadow giving him the dangerous sexy look that she loved. "And if there's serious shit coming, I want to be neck deep in it with you, honey. No ifs, ands or buts."

"Wonder Woman. I love Wonder Woman." Rafe kissed her palm. "You'd have been safer staying there, with Grandmother. She was right about that."

"When you were only the boat ride from hell away?" Lacy laughed. "How could I just wait back there like your obedient little woman when you might need me? Surely you know me better than that."

"Yeah, baby, I do." Rafe ran a hand down her back and squeezed her butt. When some of the other men whistled, he gave them a blistering stare. "I love you. If we weren't in a hell of a hurry to get this antidote, I'd take you downstairs right now and show you how much I've missed you." He kissed her silent when she started to ask him about his plans. "Later. Now go with Chica. Dry off."

"I love you too. Promise you won't leave before I get back up here." Lacy kissed him quickly before he turned to Ed. Damn it, he didn't answer her.

"Who the hell is minding the club while you're off halfway around the world?" Rafe didn't seem to care that Ed was twice his size when he got in his face and poked him in his massive chest.

Oops, time to retreat even though she wanted that promise from him. She heard Ed mumble an answer while she followed the woman. This was a big, luxurious ship. She cast another anxious glance at the darkening sky before she went below. The idea of being on the water during a storm didn't exactly fill her heart with gladness.

"You are very tall. But we have some men's things that

should work for you." Chica rummaged in a duffle bag and came out with gray sweat pants.

"Tall and still bloated from childbirth." Lacy looked over Chica's petite figure. "I hope I can trim down again. Those pants and a loose t-shirt, the looser the better, will work."

"Don't worry. I can tell you from experience that it takes time to lose the baby weight. And you carried three at once!" She grinned. "How excited Rafael was when he told us."

Lacy pulled out her phone. She and Chica spent a few minutes cooing over baby pictures. It was her knee-jerk attitude lately and she didn't apologize for it. Chica had two kids at home and pronounced Lacy's babies perfect, even using her own phone to share pictures. After that, Lacy wanted to let her mother know she was okay and to check on the babies, but getting cell reception proved impossible.

"Yes, this is a dead zone for cell and Internet service." Chica made a face. "You know, I was surprised that Rafael came home to the clan. He vowed never to return when he left." She looked away when Lacy shucked her wet clothes. "He was very bitter back then. Some of the people were unkind, you see. His mother was nasty. She didn't try to get along in the village. She lured Rafael's papa away time and time again. *Pobrecito* Rafael. He was left to be raised by his *abuela*. That means grandmother." Chica turned around. "I don't know if you speak Spanish."

"Just a little. I do live in Texas. There are a lot of people who speak it there. So I've picked up some common phrases. I can ask where the bathroom is and order food." Lacy smiled and pulled back her wet hair. She would have to get an app for her phone to help her translate some of the words Chica had tossed so casually into her conversation. "You have a rubber band for this mop?"

"Oh, no! Let me find a comb for you. It is too pretty a

color to just pull back. And Rafael will like to see it free, I think." Chica found a comb and asked Lacy to sit on a bunk. "Let me. I like to do hair."

"Thanks." Lacy relaxed as Chica carefully worked through the tangles. "You're being awfully nice to a were-cat. You do know I am one. Right?"

"Rafael has made no secret of it. Hey, he loves you. I saw that in his eyes when he noticed you coming across the water in that boat. So I accept you. And you had his children. You will forever be part of the clan now. No matter what." Chica sighed. "That is what his mother didn't understand. Rafael's birth tied her to our clan but she didn't care. To leave her little boy and him a demon…"

"What?" Lacy jerked and then winced when the comb got caught in her hair. "Rafe's a demon?" Had he ever told her that? Of course he hadn't. It wasn't the kind of thing she'd forget. Had Glory known?

"He didn't tell you?" Chica sighed. "His mother is a bad *demonio*. We are sure she put some kind of spell on Rafael's father. There is no other explanation for his leaving all he loved behind like he did. His clan, his family, his sons. It makes no sense otherwise." Chica sat beside Lacy. "Rafael hates that part of himself. He's a good man. You won't ever see him do anything, um, demon-like. I'm sure of that. Don't tell him I said anything about his mother. He doesn't talk about her."

"I can't promise that." Lacy was shaking. Rafe a demon? She'd seen some demons. Glory had suffered at their hands. Nasty didn't begin to describe their tricks and torments. Oh, God. Now her babies had some of that nastiness in them. Why hadn't she ever noticed, sensed it in Rafe? She faced Chica.

"You are sure about this. It isn't just gossip you are passing on."

"I have seen his mother, Lacy." Chica shuddered. "For Rafael's sake I wish I was wrong. But she is a *demonio* and there is no mistake about it. The red eyes, the shifting into something so evil you want to run for your life. And she can look at you and you are turned to stone." She grabbed Lacy's hand. "Can you believe it? You can't move an inch."

"I believe it. I've seen it happen." Lacy bowed her head, thinking hard. What did this mean? Could she marry a man who was half demon? And what about his acting as father to her children? Wait. There was no acting, he *was* their father. Hell and damnation. Her head swam and she sat on the bed. She'd known Rafe for a long time. Loved him for months. There'd been no sign... Sitting here with Chica wringing her hands and watching over her wasn't going to accomplish a thing.

"Thanks for telling me, Chica. I needed to know." Lacy jerked at her t-shirt which wasn't nearly as loose as she wished. She and her lover were going to have a talk. Like right now. She patted Chica's hand.

"Don't worry. I won't get you in trouble. How could you know he hadn't told me? We are practically on our way to the altar. He should have mentioned it." Damned right. Lacy headed for the door.

"You are mad. Please, take a breath. Think. Rafael has much on his mind. Don't burden him with this right now. The *puta* we are dealing with is dangerous. Rafael is going to have to confront her on his own. It is the only way to save his grandfather. If you bring another worry to him, it will distract him when he needs to be focused. *¿Entiéndeme?*" Chica was beside her now, pulling on her arm when Lacy tried to leave the cabin.

Lacy stopped and did take a breath. Okay, the woman had a point. What was this about Rafe going in alone? Were these people crazy or just cowards? She wasn't about to let her man, liar or deceptive bastard that he was, take on this *puta*, whatever that was, by himself. The woman had used poison on Rafe's grandfather. Who knew what else she was capable of?

"I get it. Calming down. I'll talk to him about this issue later. Thanks for the info." She shook off Chica's hand. "Now I'm going up. To be by his side." Lacy stomped up the stairs. When she got there, Rafe was gone. Several other people milled around, looking worried.

"Where the hell is Rafe?" Lacy confronted Ed who turned to the person standing where Rafe had been minutes before.

"He's gone to talk to Shiloh. I'm Marguerite." The woman held out her hand and Lacy shook it absently. "We tried to stop him but he wanted to get this thing moving. Matias is dying, you know, and then there's a storm brewing. Miguel, tell her. Rafael and Tomas took off as soon as she went below."

"Is Shiloh the *puta*? Take me to Rafe." Lacy stared toward the rocky land a hundred yards away. "Or am I going to have to swim to shore?" She shuddered thinking about it.

"Yes, Shiloh is the *puta*." That man who wore the captain's hat stepped up to her. Miguel. "Forget swimming. Won't do you any good. None of us are going to lead you to him. Rafael has a plan, lady. He wants to do this alone with only Tomas along to report back if he needs us."

"Lacy, these people know what they're doing." Ed tried to put his hand on her but backed away when she glared at him. "Let Rafe handle this. Tomas is his brother. He'll help him if he needs it."

"Two men? Against how many?" Lacy snarled. "Those odds suck and you know it."

"You just got here, *senorita*. Don't mess things up by going in there and catting around." The captain was obviously used to taking charge.

"I don't take orders from you." Lacy stood her ground. "Why are you letting Rafe take all the risk? Are you afraid to go over there? This man," she grabbed Ed's sleeve, "makes a mean gorilla, or so I've heard. My cat is no slouch either. I say we go after Rafe and give him back up. Help his brother if it comes to a fight. Come on, who's with me? Or do I have to swim to shore by myself?"

"She's right. Why are we standing around with our thumbs up our *culos* when Rafael is putting his life on the line? We should at least be close by if he needs us." Miguel gestured and led the way to the back of the ship. "You won't have to swim, *chica gato*. I'll lower the dingy. It'll hold six. But the rest of you can shift and we'll meet on shore. There's a path to take to their enclave. Won't hurt to be close if Rafael needs us."

"Now you're talking. You can shift into whatever beasts work best for you if it comes to a battle." Lacy swallowed when she saw them pick up dangerous looking weapons and check for extra ammunition. "Or not."

"You're right, Lacy." Chica tucked two knives into her boots and a wicked looking handgun into her belt. "I say we move out now. Rafael deserves our loyalty and support. He showed his *cojones*, *gente*, now show him yours."

In short order they were on the move. Lacy carefully climbed down into the bobbing boat. More water. But she ignored it, even helped load the shifters' weapons into the skiff. Before long they were on dry land, following one of the men who had scouted the area and could lead the way. Chica filled her in on the witch and her tactics as they walked. By the time the white fortress came into view, Lacy was terrified for Rafe. She had no idea what they'd find. The absolute quiet of the place was scarier than if they'd seen a fight going on.

CHAPTER TEN

Rafe flew into the fortress and landed in the middle of the open area before he shifted in front of a startled man who reached for his pistol.

"Take me to Shiloh." Rafe stared hard, letting his eyes go red. The man trembled in fear, dropped his gun to the ground, then led Rafe toward a small building with a wooden door. A protection symbol had been painted on the door and Rafe felt the power of it repel him. Strong but not impossible to deal with.

"Ask her to come out." He pitched his voice to a low growl. Not bad. He almost sounded like the Devil himself. He knew Tomas was listening on a roof nearby. He hated that his brother could hear him sound like that.

The man hurried to knock on the door and rushed inside when a voice told him to enter. Soon a woman stepped outside. Shiloh. She wore a sheer white shirt held together by two buttons at her waist. Her breasts were full and high and he could see them clearly through the thin material. Her gauzy skirt flowed around her legs and her feet were bare. Gold bracelets jangled on her arms and her green eyes gleamed with interest as she looked Rafe over. More gold dripped from her ears and her wavy blond hair hung down her back almost to her hips. She was small but her power made her seem larger. Rafe didn't move as she strutted toward him. He smiled, pleased when she licked her lips, her eyes bright behind thick lashes. Game on.

"Well, well. Who have we here?" She flicked a wrist and a dozen men ran out of various buildings to surround him. "You have the look of Clan Castillo. Did Matias send you?" She reached toward him with fingernails painted silver and filed sharp, as if she had weaponized them.

"Rafael Castillo. Matias is my grandfather." Rafe bowed but kept out of reach. He wasn't stupid. If she was indeed a witch, she could do plenty of harm with a simple touch. Of course there were guns pointed at him that could do more damage. He hoped Tomas stayed where he was, out of range.

"And how is my lover? Why isn't he here himself?" She pouted prettily. "He has been neglecting me lately."

"Perhaps that's because my grandfather is dead." Rafe continued to stare at her, not even blinking while she put on a show of screeching and tearing at her hair.

"No, you are lying. My beloved! He cannot be dead. How did it happen?" She fell to the stones, her face in her hands. He was supposed to believe that she was weeping.

Rafe wasn't fooled. He doubted she'd shed a single tear. "Poison. Very unusual for our kind to be susceptible to such a thing, don't you think? But then I hear concocting potent brews is a specialty of yours."

Her head snapped up. "Poison? Are you accusing *me* of this?"

"I have heard it is one of your talents." Rafe saw her men move closer when he put his hand on the knife at his hip.

"Why would I hurt the man I loved?" She tossed her hair. "You are mad."

Rafe drew his knife and took a step closer. He wasn't surprised when two men grabbed his arms. It was a move he'd anticipated.

"You dare come here to attack me?" Her hiss of anger burned like acid against his chest. Her men moved in but she stopped them with a gesture. She murmured one of her spells and waited for it to work on him.

Rafe felt her magic hit him like an invisible sledge hammer but he withstood its power. He smiled and shook his head. "Is that all you've got?"

"Shoot him!" Shiloh backed away and stamped her foot. The men opened fire but Rafe used the two men holding him as shields and they both were hit.

"Stop!" Shiloh shrieked. "You're killing our own men!" She batted at the air when an eagle swooped from the sky, its talons going for her eyes. She murmured some words and waved her hands and the eagle dropped to the ground, stunned. "Who is this?"

Rafe knew who it was. Tomas to the rescue. Only he'd just complicated things.

"Never mind that. Call off your men or you'll be sorry." Rafe let his eyes go red and threw the two dead men at a couple of others who'd decided to move in.

Shiloh laughed but raised a hand. "Stop. This is getting interesting. What are you trying to pull?" She put her foot on the bird, stopping just short of stepping down hard and breaking the eagle's neck.

"Follow through on that and I'll make sure there's not enough left of this clan to feed carrion." Rafe turned to the men nearest him and froze them in place. He knew Shiloh could see what was happening. By the time every last man was a statue, she'd stepped back from Tomas.

"What are you?" She was still not afraid. Stupid bitch. "Are you the grandson with demon blood? The one Matias complained about?"

"Watch and see." Rafe could feel the change beginning. Scales began to form on his arms and legs, while his fingers lengthened and his nails grew into claws. The horns on his head punched through his skull with a painful shudder.

"Demon. Yes." She kept watching his transformation as he grew too big for his shirt and his jeans split at the seams. "Are you now head of your clan, *mi buen hombre*?"

"I am not your anything." Rafe could feel the evil coming off of her in waves. "But you are right. I *am* taking over the clan."

"Well now. Perhaps we should go to my rooms and talk about this." She walked toward her place, her hips swaying.

"Talk? Is that truly what you wish to do?" Rafe waited to see her next move. When Shiloh turned, he looked her over, letting his demon eyes glow red for her. Her gasp was very satisfying. He was now more monster than man and, surprisingly, Shiloh wasn't afraid of him. He turned and ordered the men he'd frozen to get inside their homes. They muttered "Hail, Marys" then scurried away.

"Those are my men you just sent running for cover. Cowards, praying to their saints. Like that would help them against a monster from Hell." Shiloh stalked back to face him and ran a fingernail down his chest, drawing blood. She licked a drop from her finger and smiled. "Demon blood. Unexpectedly delicious. It almost makes me wish I was a vampire." Shiloh smiled, raking him with a hot look. "Will my protection spell keep you out of my home?"

"Not if I really, really want inside. If we were to get into a power struggle? There would be no contest." Rafe strode toward her. She started to argue, clearly used to being top bitch wherever she went. But then he let more of his demon out, growing taller as his legs lengthened and his bare feet grew their own claws. He heard more seams pop on his jeans and saw Shiloh lick her lips again when she saw the bulge behind his zipper.

Obviously the lady got off to dangerous. What form did she take when she shifted? Dragon? Griffin? Something ugly and powerful no doubt. He sure as hell didn't want to see it.

"Why are you here, Rafael? To kill me?" Shiloh jumped in front of him, scratching a nail down his chest again, his shirt falling away completely as his shoulders grew even wider and stronger. "Do you really think you can?"

"You poisoned my grandfather." Rafe stomped toward her when she backed away from him. "I see you aren't bothering to deny it. Poor Shiloh, I heard he refused to leave my grandmother for you."

"What he saw in that ancient hag, I'll never know." She edged around the clearing away from him but looked more excited than afraid.

"You punished him well, didn't you? But how could killing him help you, eh? No Castillo is going to allow you to invade our clan." Rafe grabbed her wrist, twisting until she gasped. "What's next, Shiloh? Do you think to mate with the next leader? Even if it's a demon?" He gestured at the buildings that were little more than huts. "I'm sure being near the glamour of Santa Cruz would suit you better than this hovel."

"Ah, I see you are much smarter than Matias. He didn't understand me at all. Which is why he had to go." Shiloh leaned in, trying to get closer, a move he denied with his strong grip on her arms. "He never took advantage of the island. I'm sure there are many in your clan who would have stayed if Matias had bothered to move his headquarters to one of the hotels. The penthouse suite, of course. It is beautiful and he could well afford it."

"Grandfather liked his privacy. Santa Cruz is too crowded now, with too many mortals for his peace of mind. He would never have set up shop there." Rafe could see what Shiloh had been after. When he'd arrived in Santa Cruz, he'd been shocked at the change in the sedate little island he'd left centuries before. Now it was a rich man's paradise, full of high-end hotels and luxurious getaways for jet-setters with a modern airport. Grandfather had made a fortune with his banana plantations, even starting a winery, but he'd sold off land close to the city, keeping the clan itself isolated in the mountains. It was a mistake that might yet cost Matias his life.

"It finally became clear to me that Matias wasn't open to change. Good riddance, I say." Shiloh watched Rafe closely. "You aren't like your grandfather, are you? I can see it. You will be a wise leader, clever." She wrenched at her arm. "You don't want to kill me, Rafael. I have a better idea. We will be a great team and wonderful lovers."

"But killing you would make my demon very happy." Rafe growled, long and low.

"I'm sure it would. But I see a future for us, together. There is no limit to the power we would wield. With both of us using the dark arts..." She laughed and finally wiggled away from him when he released her in disgust. "Let me prove I can work with you. I will set your eagle friend free." She stalked over to Tomas, murmured an incantation and the bird roused. It quickly looked around then took flight. It was soon out of sight, either hidden or going for reinforcements.

"Does that make you happy?" Shiloh twirled her skirt. "Can you imagine what a pair we will make?" She threw out her hands and thunder roared.

Rafe cast a glance at the sky. She would probably take credit but there were storm clouds moving in. He needed to hurry this along.

"The bird was just a bird. But I suppose knowing a few spells could be useful. What makes you think I need such as you to help run my clan?" He grabbed her hair and jerked her face inches from his. "You want to show off powers? How do you like this?" He glanced at a nearby table and it burst into flames.

She laughed. "I love it. You are setting me on fire, Rafael." She scored his cheek with her nails, drawing blood again. "Of course you don't need me, but I think you *want* me." She pulled his hand to her breast, gasping when he dug a claw into it. "Yes."

"I already have a woman. Will you poison her if she

gets in your way?" Rafe shoved her to the ground.

"Try me. See what I can do to you and for you in bed. That other woman will seem dull after I get through with you, I guarantee it. I won't have to poison her. You will send her away." She glared at men who'd come out of their houses and were trying to put out the burning table. "Leave us. Let it burn. You can get another." The men scurried inside, pulling their curious women and children with them.

"You give up things easily and your clan is full of cowards. I am not a man who throws away what he has without a fight." Rafe let more of his demon out, his voice becoming deeper and his mouth filling with fangs.

"You are making me crazy with your changes. It's as if *el diablo* himself has come calling and I love it." She gasped when Rafe grabbed her hair and pulled her toward her house. "Are you reading my mind? I love pain and a man who knows how to use it to give me what I want. This night will be one of endless pleasure. You will see."

"I see that you are a greedy bitch." Rafe roared as he let his demon take over. The ground shook and the wooden gate into the enclave burst into flames. Then a pile of crates beside it caught. The fire started spreading to some of the outbuildings but no one came to put out the flames.

"Greedy? Of course I am. I want everything. More money, more power, more people to do my bidding. And a lover who will make me scream." She licked her lips. "Go ahead burn it all down. Santa Cruz is where we belong. Together." She stared up at him hungrily. "There are no limits to what we will accomplish." She shrieked with laughter, sounding more than a little insane. "You can't know how happy I am to finally meet a man worthy of me."

"I've heard that many have had you. They call you *puta*, whore. Easy to have but not to hold. Will you tire of me and send me to hell like you did Matias? I warn you now that I won't go down without taking you with me." Rafe kept dragging her toward that painted door. Her eyes were sparkling, no fear in them at all. She was waiting to see if her protection spell could keep him out.

"I can see you will be different. A demon! But are you strong enough for me? Are you, Rafael?" She giggled when he kicked open her door and stalked inside, ducking to keep from hitting the door frame.

"Satisfied, Shiloh? Clearly your paltry protection spell couldn't keep me out." Rafe dropped her on the oriental carpet and looked around. There was a work table against one wall but he had no idea which bottle or jar might hold the right potion.

"Paltry? It was a special spell. That you could walk through it makes me sure we are meant to be together. I am on fire for you. Take me to bed. Fuck me until I can't stand." Shiloh ripped open her blouse and tore at her skirt. "Shall I shift or do you want me in this form? You should see what else I can be. It will amaze you."

"Be still, woman. I will let you know what I want, when I want it." Rafe's growl worked. Shiloh stopped what she was doing and stared at him worshipfully, clearly ready to do his bidding. "First, give me the poison you used on Matias and the antidote. I have an enemy I want to make sure dies a painful death. Like my grandfather did." Rafe forced a laugh. "That was well done of you. His agony was a thing of beauty. You are very clever."

"Yes, I am. It took me a long time to get the formula just right. So a shifter would die from it." Shiloh preened for a moment then shook her head. "But it is *my* special brew, Rafael. I am the only one who should--"

Rafe swung his fist, barely missing her face and knocking over a table. "I don't have to listen to this, woman. Do as I say!" He turned and kicked more of her furniture, turning the room into a shambles. A cask of jewels flew across the room, scattering diamonds, rubies and emerald jewelry everywhere. He stalked over to a closet and began to rip clothing apart before turning to look at her. She had picked up some of her necklaces, but still watched him avidly. "What are you waiting for? The poison, Shiloh. Or do you want to put off our pleasure all night?"

"No, no! I want you inside me. I am dying for you. I am sure you are hung like a *toro*."

"There's only one way to find out." Rafe gave her a look that made her hurry to the table against the wall and pull open a drawer.

She fumbled two vials into a bag. "The red is the poison, the yellow the antidote. I always make sure I have a cure. In case I have to take some of the poison when I am ridding myself of a pest. Matias was easy to fool into taking the poisoned drink. He was so fond of his wine he never even sniffed his glass." She laughed and set the bag by the door.

Rafe just nodded. He couldn't trust himself to say a single word or he'd tell her exactly what he really thought of her.

Shiloh kicked away the last of her clothes and threw herself on the bed. She held out her arms. "I did what you wanted. Now, please, please take me. I need you." She wiggled with delight. "A demon lover. This will be a night to remember for both of us."

Rafe stared at her. He'd met many sinful people in his long life. This woman had no morality, not an ounce. He knew he should end her. But, demon or not, he'd never been a cold-blooded killer. He stalked over to stand next to the bed. She lay spread out invitingly, offering herself to him with an eager smile. The man in him noticed every detail of her voluptuous body. Then there was the darkness of her soul. His demon recognized it, even reveled in the pure evil that came off of her in waves. He despised the fact that he was as hard as a fence post.

"You are so like your grandfather. But he lacked the edge, the taste for sin that I wanted and needed. Come here, demon. Fuck me until I scream for mercy but don't you dare give it to me." She ran a sharp fingernail down his stomach to the waistband of his jeans and flicked it open. "Let me see your magnificence." Shiloh reached for his cock, pulling down his zipper and grasping him. She laughed and ran a nail along his length, proving again that she was into pain and blood. It was all Rafe could do not to break her neck then and there.

"Yes, I knew you would be like this." She tried to lift her head, as if to take him with her mouth.

Rafe couldn't bear the thought and stopped her with a hand on her forehead. "Be still, woman, or this will be over before it's begun."

She smiled up at him but did lay back and even release him. "Relax, demon. We have all night, don't we? It will be amazing." She ran her hands over her own body, touching the places where she wanted him to touch her.

Rafe wanted to run like hell. He had the antidote. He could leave. But what about Shiloh? Would she make another attempt to take over the clan? He had no desire to stay here and play bodyguard. He didn't say a word just stood there, trying to bring himself to do what he knew he had to do.

"Why do you hesitate, demon?" Shiloh reached for him, sliding her hands over his hips and urging him closer. "I can tell that you will fill me. Give me children. We will rule the world!" She tried to pull him down on top of her. "First we must rid ourselves of Iliana, of course. That crone should have gone centuries ago."

His grandmother. Of course this bitch would have a kill list. Decision made, Rafe reached for her face as if he was about to kiss her. Then, using both hands, he grasped her head. There was only one way to rid the world of such evil. Her clan would thank him for doing what had to be done.

"Say hello to the Devil, Shiloh." With a swift and powerful move, he twisted, then jerked off her head and flung it to the floor. He didn't waste time looking at the bloody bed clothes or her slack body. Nor did he celebrate ridding the world of a malevolent being. He just turned, grabbed the bag by the door, and walked out of the house.

The air was full of smoke and fire was about to reach one of the houses. He shouted.

"Fire! Get your asses out here and put out these fires before you lose your homes! Shiloh is dead. Elect a new leader." He kicked aside the charred front gate and marched out. No one bothered to follow him. The people were too busy trying to save their village. Tomas landed next to him, shifting quickly. He eyed him warily and kept several feet between them.

"You get what we need, bro?"

"Yes. Take it. Thanks for trying to help. You did well." Rafe thrust the bag at him as he struggled to get out of his demon form. He couldn't pull himself back to human until he calmed down. Adrenaline coursed through his body, his heart pounded and he was about to jump out of his scaly skin. He looked down and saw his hands covered in Shiloh's blood.

"Rafe?"

God help him. He knew that voice. When she saw him like this, the woman he loved would never love him again. What the hell could he do to ever make this right with her?

Lacy wasn't sure how she recognized the monster standing in the middle of the path. Maybe it was something about how he stood-- legs apart, arms strong and ready for a fight. He wasn't making a move toward them either, the Castillo shifters armed to the teeth.

It couldn't be his smell. That was mostly wood smoke and ... blood. He was huge, dark green and covered with scales. His hands, if you could call them that, ended in enormous claws. Those were bloody. She didn't want to think about why. Toes had claws too. When he opened his mouth, as if to speak, she could see rows of sharp teeth, almost like the fangs vampires had but dozens of them. Then there were his horns...

God, there was hardly anything human about him. She took a breath then swallowed. He was the ugliest, most disgusting, and scariest thing she'd ever seen in her life. It took everything in her not to turn tail and run for her life.

"Lacy." He said her name in a deep growl that was almost a moan.

Definitely Rafe. She shivered and couldn't help herself. She turned and ran. She morphed into her cat, a big red and white because she could run a hell of a lot faster that way. She'd memorized the route back to the ship and the small boat that would get her there. The shifters could do their bird thing to get back as far as she was concerned. She was not going to stand around and talk to Rafe while he looked like that. No way in hell.

Someone or something was following her. When a hand clamped down on her tail, she skidded to a stop. She couldn't afford to let some idiot damage that part of her. A glance over her shoulder showed her that a rapidly changing Rafe was the idiot. At least it was a hand now holding her and not those damned claws, though he was still bloody.

"Let go. If you hurt my tail I could end up incontinent. How would you like to change my diapers for the rest of our lives?" Lacy twitched when he wouldn't let go. "God damn it, Rafe, release me so I can change back." She glanced down the path. No one else was in sight. That was a blessing anyway.

"Are you going to stick around and let me explain?" He sounded more like himself too. His scales were fading. But he was still sporting a really awesome chest, twice as big as usual. His clothes were in bits and pieces so that he was next to naked. Thank God the horns had disappeared.

"Break my tail and it would forever drag the ground. I wasn't kidding about the incontinence thing either. It could happen. And if it had to be amputated?" Lacy heard her voice rise. "Well, bud, I'd lose some of my balance. Might not ever jump on the back of a couch or roof again without falling off. See my point? Why I'm pissed at you right now?"

"Okay, okay. Sorry." He dropped her tail and held out his hands.

Lacy shifted back into her human form and took off running again. He wanted her to stand around and talk? After what she'd just seen? Fuck him. Liar. And she hadn't missed the fact that he'd come back from his meeting with the infamous poisoner with a giant hard-on. She wanted to kill him.

She was a fast runner and he was either having a problem recovering from his demon thing or maybe he'd wised up and figured out she needed a cooling off period. Whatever. She arrived alone at the small boat they'd pulled up onto the shore. One of the men in Rafe's clan stood guard over it.

"I need to go back to the ship. Can you help me?" She started shoving at the boat.

"We should wait for the others." The man looked anxiously down the path. "What happened?"

"Rafe handled it. He's a demon, you know. Last thing I saw was the woman's headquarters on fire. Guess Rafe got the poison and antidote from her." Lacy closed her eyes, picturing him on that trail. "Oh, and he was covered in blood. Since he didn't seem hurt, I think he must have taken her out."

"¡*Estupendo*!" The man still didn't help her push the boat into the water. "So we wait. To take the antidote and the weapons back to the ship. We must get the cure to Matias as soon as possible."

"Oh, fine!" Lacy pulled off her baggy sweat pants and, steeling herself, jumped into the cold water. She could sort of swim. It wasn't anything she'd wanted to learn but her mother had insisted her children know the survival skill. So she did a cat paddle through the salty water, going under a few times and sputtering when she accidentally swallowed the gross salty stuff.

Finally she reached the boat, exhausted, wet and barely able to reach the chrome diving platform at the back of the ship. She climbed on it and lay there for a while trying to catch her breath. The wind had picked up and she shivered, forced to move her butt and go on up the ladder onto the deck. A crewman helped her over the railing and handed her a towel. Lacy staggered below, praying Chica's bag held another pair of sweats. She was eyeing the shower when she heard a shout from up above. The group in the boat had arrived. Thumps over her head assured her they were on board.

Fine. Let them celebrate. The ship's engine started and the boat lurched into motion. Clearly they were in a hurry. Oh, yeah. Matias needed that antidote. Feeling more than a little ashamed of forgetting the urgency, Lacy shut herself inside the tiny bathroom and turned on the shower. Hot water. It felt wonderful and washed away the sticky salt from her body and her hair. She felt more like herself when she finally emerged with a towel wrapped around her. Of course she wasn't alone. Rafe lay on the double bed. He'd obviously found another shower because all he wore was a solemn look.

CHAPTER ELEVEN

"I'd appreciate it if you'd cover yourself." Lacy turned away from him, clearly disgusted by what she'd seen earlier. Disgusted by *him*.

Rafe sat up, trying to figure out how he could possibly make this right. Of course he should have told her about his demon blood early in their relationship. But how do you drop that kind of thing into casual conversation? "Oh, hey, I'm half demon. And did you remember to get milk at the grocery store?" Yeah, right.

"Lacy, would you look at me?" He did pull the sheet up to his waist.

"If you think we're just going to kiss and make up, think again." She did peek at him from where she rummaged in a duffel bag. Probably just to make sure he'd done as she'd asked. "I can't believe what I saw back there."

"No wonder you ran. You figure out what I was? Am?" Rafe couldn't just lie there when Lacy was about to lose her towel. Her creamy skin was flushed, from her face to the swells of her breasts above the towel she reached to tighten. Damn. He hated that she'd been caught off guard about his demon like that.

"Yes, Rafe. I'm not stupid. Glory had to face some of those things not all that long ago. Plus Chica had already let slip that your mother was a demon. Nice genes you've got there, Rafe. I can't believe I've been living with you all this time and I didn't have a clue that you're a freaking demon." Lacy stepped into a pair of baggy sweat pants then pulled a huge sweatshirt over her head. It must have belonged to Ed because four of her could have fit in it. "Guess I *am* stupid after all."

"No, of course you're not. I keep that part of me well hidden. It's not something I'm proud of." Rafe wrapped the sheet around him and crawled off the bed to stand in front of Lacy when he saw he had her full attention.

"Did Glory know?" She was rigid with anger. "Answer me!"

"Yes. You know Glory went to church on Sunday nights. I couldn't go inside. Gave me the shakes and worse. The demon blood does that." Rafe could see that revelation made Lacy swallow. They'd never discussed religion. The cats seemed to have their own version of worship and he'd never had to confront a church door with her. Thank God the wedding they'd attended had been outdoors.

"So how'd your mother end up with a member of your clan?" Lacy sat on the foot of the bed.

"My father met her more than a thousand years ago and fell under her spell. He couldn't resist her, still can't." Rafe didn't try to hide his bitterness. There had been many times when he'd wished he'd never been born. "I'm proof of my father's weakness. I've spent a long lifetime trying to live down my demon ancestry. I'm the clan's shameful secret."

"Your grandparents don't seem to think so. They sent for you, didn't they?" She flinched when he moved closer, like she'd freak if he touched her.

"Because they were desperate. Sometimes having a demon in the family comes in handy. It did tonight. I got the antidote for Grandfather. Maybe it will save him. I hope to God it will." Rafe felt helpless in the face of her fear. Did he blame her for feeling blindsided? Of course not. But somehow he had to get through to her and remind her that she'd loved him before...

"That's good, Rafe. That you got the antidote." She was obviously having trouble reconciling what she'd seen tonight with the Rafe she'd known, slept with, started a family with.

At least Rafe knew Lacy was nothing if not fair. He'd seen her work with some pretty strange characters before, giving them her friendship when others might have shunned them. Because she and her boss Glory welcomed paranormals of all stripes into Glory's shop, the place had become a haven for outcasts. Rafe realized that he'd joined that club in her eyes. But at least she didn't shrink from him as he edged closer.

"I can't help what I am, Lacy, any more than you can change what you are. I've spent my entire life trying to prove that I don't have to let my evil half rule me." He sat beside her, close enough that he could feel her stiffen. "Do you believe me?"

"I, I saw you in a monster's skin. You scared the shit out of me, Rafe. If there was an ounce of humanity in you then, I sure didn't see it." She stood and stepped out of reach. "I'm used to shape-shifters. But that was... unholy."

"I know. And I wouldn't have unleashed that tonight if it hadn't been the only way to deal with Shiloh." Rafe ran his hand across his face. Would she ever be able to get the picture of his demon out of her head? "I hate changing into that thing. Yes, that's what it is, a thing. I turn into my mother's child then. Connected to hell in a way I don't want to be. Ever." He saw Lacy frown. "But I would never hurt you or our children. I'd die first. Do you believe me?"

"Are you sure you can always control it?" She bit her lip. "You didn't seem completely yourself back there, no matter what you say."

109

Rafe wasn't about to admit she was right. That kind of oversharing would send her running from him forever.

"In all the time you've known me, have you ever seen me act the demon before?"

Lacy sighed and sat next to him again. "No. You're right. You're a good man, Rafe, or I'd never have fallen in love with you in the first place."

"Thank you." Rafe sighed and pulled her into his arms. "Please, please believe me when I say that all I want is to be a man who deserves you and our children."

"What *about* our children?" She looked into his eyes. "Are they going to be turning into monsters someday?"

"I have no idea. But if one of them shows signs of the demon in him or her, like I did when I was growing up? Well, we'll deal with it. I'm proof positive that a good role model can make even a half demon become a decent person. My grandfather made sure I knew right from wrong." Rafe hugged Lacy close, wishing he could promise her that none of the babies would manifest any evil whatsoever. "At least our children will only have inherited a quarter of their DNA from hell." He soothed her with a hand down her back. "I'm sorry I didn't tell you long ago. Should have before we hit the sheets the first time. But I never thought you'd get pregnant. My stupidity. I'd hung around vampires too long and they can't--"

"I know. Can't have children." Lacy shook her head. "I was stupid too. Birth control. Every cat knows how to prevent pregnancy. I didn't bother. We both got carried away. We have such awesome chemistry…"

"Yes, we do." Rafe tilted her face up to give her a deep kiss. Chemistry. But it wasn't just that. He had a connection with this woman on many levels. They laughed together, played together and had many of the same values. He said as much to her.

"You're right. And I know you'll be an awesome father to our children. That's a big deal to me. My own father was absent much of the time. My mom calls him a tomcat.

In our cat family that's the worst."

"Well, you can take this to the bank— I'll never abandon my children. That's what my dad did to me and I suffered for it." Rafe ran his hands under her shirt. "Baby, I've missed you so much."

"Mmm." Lacy held onto him and kissed him until he started pulling her down on the bed. "Wait a minute." She shoved his hands off of her. "I need to know what happened, Rafe. With that woman. The leader of that clan." Lacy brushed off his hands when he tried to pull her back to him. "No, don't try to distract me. You came back from Shiloh covered with blood and, damn it, you were turned on!" She looked him over.

Well, hell, of course he was turned on now too. He'd lost his sheet so there was no way to hide that. Being close to his woman, tasting her and feeling her body against his, even through that heavy sweatshirt fabric, had made him desperate to bury himself in Lacy's sweet body and cleanse himself of that horrific meeting with his grandfather's mistress.

"Quit thinking and start talking, Rafe." Lacy had her hands on her hips.

Rafe knew better than to smile. But she looked so entirely fuckable, issuing orders, sure she could make him do whatever she wanted. And she was so right. He'd tell her everything.

"Sit on the bed and I'll start." Rafe sat and patted the bed beside him.

"Talking, nothing else until I'm satisfied that you've left nothing out." She was suspicious as she settled next to him, a foot between them.

"Fine." He closed his eyes. Shit but he hated to relive those moments. But he did, telling Lacy every single detail. "So you see, Shiloh admitted everything. She bragged about poisoning Grandfather. She was sure she and I could rule the world, take over clan after clan of shifters if we worked together."

111

Lacy laid her hand on his knee. "How horrible. You say you think she was a witch?"

"Yes. She had some skills. She was impressed by my demon. That's why I had to change." He picked up Lacy's hand and squeezed. "I hated to do it. I was shifting back when you saw me on the trail. The blood..." He dropped her hand and stared at the floor. "I took her head, Lacy. It was the only way to stop her."

"You killed her." Lacy dropped to her knees in front of him. "It was the right thing to do, Rafe. If she'd lived, who knows how many other people she would have hurt?"

"That's why I did it." Rafe looked into her eyes. She didn't hate him. And wasn't that a miracle. "About my arousal..."

"Forget it. I know men. You can't control it. I'm sure she did everything she could to make you want her. And I bet she was beautiful." She narrowed her gaze. "If anything happened between you, I don't want to know about it."

He pulled her up and into his lap. "Nothing did, baby. I love you. I still can't believe you rode in a fucking speedboat across the Atlantic to be with me. That was totally hot."

"Glad you think so. I was terrified." She smoothed her hand across his bare shoulder. "I do love you. For a cat, what I did to see you proves it." She wiggled in his lap and ran her hand through his hair. "Now I think we've talked enough. Will you take me to bed and make love to me?"

"My brave cat, risking death by drowning. Just when I thought I couldn't love you more." Rafe kissed her, savoring their connection.

"Remind me of the good things we have and get that picture of the monster you turned into out of my head." She leaned her head against his chest and inhaled, her eyes closed. "Rafael. I love the way everyone here calls you that. It sounds so sexy."

"A challenge. I'm up for it." Rafe pushed his hand

under her sweatshirt and cupped her breast. "But are you sure lovemaking is a good idea? You just gave birth. You can't have recovered from that yet."

"I was examined by Ian before I left Austin. He says I have remarkable healing powers. It's a were-cat thing. If I want to have sex now, I'm good to go." She kissed his chin. "No excuses, you making love to me now or not?"

"Of course." Rafe met her lips in a long kiss then leaned back and shook his head. "But you can't know how insane it makes me to think of that vampire 'examining' you, sweetheart."

"It was clinical. Nothing to it. Trust me, if Ian had so much as waggled an eyebrow when he checked me, I'd have scratched his eyes out." Lacy held on when Rafe stood with her in his arms. "Oh, guess that means you're ready."

"I've been ready since I saw your red hair flying like a flag in that boat coming toward me earlier." Rafe leaned down and kissed her again with everything in him. God, how he loved this woman. That she could accept him, demon and all, blew him away. He walked to the bed and laid her down then sat beside her. "But no matter what you say, I'm being careful. Three babies! Popping them out can't have been easy."

"I never said it was easy. They didn't just 'pop out'." Lacy pulled her shirt off over her head and threw it across the room. Her pants went next.

"My turn now. I want every detail." Rafe couldn't get enough of just looking at her when she lay naked next to him and stretched, so sensual and gorgeous she took his breath.

"Trust me, no you don't. I'll give you the highlights." She brushed her hand across his chest, teasing a nipple. "I pushed for hours. Screamed your name and cursed you so loud that Ian had to order his bodyguards to stand down. They thought you'd breached his security." She pinched him, just enough to make him wince.

"God, I'm sorry." Rafe smoothed a hand over her stomach, horrified at the thought of what she'd been through. And of course he hadn't been there for her.

"You should be sorry. I wanted you there for the miracle of their births." She smiled and tugged at his hair. "Bet you would have cried along with them, my man. It was a beautiful, wonderful thing." She laughed at the look on his face.

Rafe didn't doubt he might have shed a tear or two. God, he'd never understand this woman. "How can I ever make it up to you?"

"Ah, exactly what I wanted to hear." Her smile was wicked. "You owe me, lover. If I say don't go easy, I mean it. I want all you've got, Rafael. Now!" She grabbed his shoulders and pulled him on top of her.

"Can I at least do this first?" He grinned and ran a hand over her breast, tweaking her nipple. "You have a problem with a little foreplay?" He followed his hand with his mouth, running his tongue over her until she squirmed under him.

"Hmm, okay. And talk dirty to me in Spanish. I want the full Latin lover treatment." She stroked his back, then clutched his buttocks. "I have missed you so damned much."

Rafe murmured some raunchy words in his native language then leaned down to take her earlobe in his teeth, biting down gently. His hands were busy finding those places he knew were her most sensitive.

"Ooo, yeah. That's what I'm talking about." Her nails dug into him and she ran a foot up the back of his calf. "I'm not sure I can handle too much foreplay. I've been wet since you kissed me on deck when I got here."

"Hmm. Let me check that out." Rafe rolled them over until she was on sprawled on top of him. Then he slid a finger inside her. "Yes, indeed. I think you--" He stopped when he heard her gasp. "Am I hurting you, Lacy? I swear, if this is too soon…"

"No!" She sat up and grabbed his cock, guiding him into her. "Come on, Rafe. I swear I'm going to die if you don't--" She moaned when he gently eased inside. "Oh, God, but I needed that. Yes, all the way. Don't you dare hold back even an inch."

Rafe held onto her slim hips, still afraid this was too soon and he'd hurt her. But she'd have none of his careful handling. She snarled at him and raised her hips then slammed down, taking him all the way to her core. Then she threw back her head, tossing her hair and howling her pleasure.

"Lacy, honey, stop it. I can't--" Rafe worried that she felt too tight. What if he tore her? She'd told him in one of their phone calls that she'd had stitches. Could she really be totally healed?

She glared down at him and began to move. "You fuck me hard, Rafael Castillo. I mean it." She shook her head. "Oh, yeah, another reason for me to be mad as hell at you. That last name. Were you ever going to tell me your real one? You asked me to marry you. What name would I take? Huh?" She shuddered, her eyes closed for a moment. When he didn't move she glared down at him. "Move, damn it! Fuck me hard now or I swear I'm taking the next plane home as soon as we hit Santa Cruz."

"Fine. But you tell me to stop if this hurts." Rafe winced when she slammed down on him again. Lacy had never been into pain before. What the hell was this about?

She slapped his face and it wasn't a love tap. "Shut up and fuck, Rafael." She leaned forward then, brushing her breasts over his chest before bracing one hand on his shoulder so she could kiss him, angrily, with teeth and tongue. She was pissed and taking it out on his body.

Rafe didn't mind it. He held onto her hips and finally set the rhythm himself so he could force her to ease up. He kept one hand on her hip and another on her breast and kissed *her* this time. He teased with his tongue until her mouth relaxed and she gave him what he wanted, the kind of kiss they shared when they made love with pure pleasure.

He knew what she liked and this new aggressive Lacy was going to have to calm the hell down. Her orgasm was about to shudder through her, he knew the signs. She dug her claws into his arms, arched her back and growled like she was about to shift into her cat. He knew she wouldn't but it would be a near thing when he took her over the edge.

He rolled again, sliding her under him so he could look down at her when she came. He loved to see her look of bliss when that happened. He moved a hand down to find her swollen clit. A stroke of his fingertip and she howled.

"Rafe!" She held his sacs in her hand, squeezing, squeezing as if to punish him. He could take it. His own release thundered through him.

"I love you, Lacy." Rafe pushed into her one last time, holding onto her so that she got every last bit of him. They shuddered together and he felt her toenails rip a path up his legs.

"God help me but I love you too, Rafael." She sobbed against his neck, clearly spent as she held him tightly. "You demon bastard. I don't know why I'm forgiving you. Promise me. No more secrets."

Rafe pushed back her tangled hair and rubbed away tears from her flushed cheeks. "Look at me, Lacy." He waited until her eyes met his. Glorious eyes, the color of new grass. Did she have secrets? He knew better than to ask.

CHAPTER TWELVE

"I promise. No more secrets." He pulled out from her and lay back so she could rest on his chest.

"Thank you." She purred as she stroked his stomach. Her fingers circled his navel. "I know I was a bitch to you."

"Feel free to mistreat me like that any time." Rafe kissed the top of her head. "But are you sure you're okay? You were rough on yourself, not just me." He sat up and looked her over. Was that blood streaking her thighs? He got up and went into the bathroom, wetting a washcloth. "Baby, you're bleeding."

"It's normal. I need some feminine products." She flushed and glanced at the door. "It's what happens after childbirth since I'm not nursing anymore. I'll have to ask Chica."

Rafe went back into the bathroom and came out with a box of tampons. "Will this do?"

"I'll shower first. And the answer to your question is that I'm fine. How about you? I got a little carried away." She got up and walked around him. "Your legs are bleeding."

"My wildcat." He pulled her to him and kissed her

hungrily. Finally he brushed her hair back from her face and smiled. "I'm just surprised someone didn't come to check on us. The clan is taking my word for it that you're okay. For all they know you're another Shiloh, out to kill another potential clan leader." Rafe followed Lacy into the bathroom. He turned on the shower, adjusting the temperature. "Of course I wouldn't be a popular choice anyway. That look at my demon earlier sealed the deal."

"Clan leader? You?" Lacy stepped into the small shower stall.

Rafe realized there was no way two of them could fit into the tiny stall so he sat on the closed toilet while she washed off. When she got out and dried off, he jumped in for a quick rinse.

"Rafe, answer me. Are you thinking of staying in the Canary Islands and leading the clan?" Lacy left the bathroom to pick up the sweat pants again.

"It will never happen, Lacy. My grandfather expected it, but he'll still run the clan now that we have the antidote." Rafe left her alone in the bathroom for some privacy. When she came out, she was dressed and frowning.

"What if he doesn't make it?"

"Then either my grandmother takes over or Tomas should be the leader." Rafe had wrapped a towel around his waist. His clothes were in another cabin. "The clan would never accept a demon in charge. Besides, I know we shouldn't live this far from your family. It wouldn't be fair."

"To who? Me? The children?" Lacy sat on the bed then jumped up again. It was a mess and she quickly made it up until you couldn't tell they'd just acted out a scene from a hot novel there.

"Both. If the kids turn out to be cats, they need to be raised near a family of were-cats. And I've been away from the clan too long to suddenly come in and take over now. Even if the demon thing wasn't a factor." Rafe thought about how the village had looked. Someone needed to step up though. He hated how things had gone so far downhill. He and his grandfather needed to have a serious talk. With Shiloh gone, maybe *Abuelo* would stick close to home now anyway. His brush with death should convince him that his priorities needed adjusting.

"Well, I don't want you to sacrifice your heritage for us." Lacy bit her lip. "Maybe there's a compromise."

"Baby, I turned my back on the clan long ago. Did you look at the other people with you when I showed up in my demon form earlier? Horrified is an understatement. I left in the first place because they hated my demon side. I was bullied, taunted, and treated like a second class citizen." Rafe wasn't about to share all of the things he'd put up with as a child. He decided then and there he'd never tell his children about their demon heritage. Not unless... No, surely they would be untainted.

"That's terrible!" She rushed to put her arms around him. "Surely, after what you did for them tonight, all that will change."

"Don't count on it, Lacy. I did what I had to for my grandfather. He was always decent to me. But the rest of the clan, except for my brothers and a few cousins, are very wary of me. Of demons in general. Who can blame them for that?" Rafe held onto his woman. He took comfort in her warmth, her acceptance. It was a miracle to him.

Rafe wanted to make sure Lacy understood the clan attitude. "We've seen those demons who gave Glory hell. My mother is one of the worst. Can you blame people for wanting to get me out of the clan? They had no idea how much of her depravity I would eventually manifest. Trust me, what I did tonight was all well and good, but it wasn't nearly enough to buy my acceptance."

"That's not right." She looked ready to face off with the lot of them.

"Maybe not, but it's reality." Rafe kissed her and left her to find his clothes.

119

He saw Chica with a hair dryer enter Lacy's cabin as he headed for the deck. His brother surrounded by the others. Tomas had the shifters spellbound as he described the scene with Shiloh.

"I tell you, Rafael was outnumbered but he stood up against all of them. Then he dragged that bitch by her hair to her house. That was after he set half the village on fire with just a look."

"Not quite half the village, *hermano.*" Rafe stepped up beside Tomas. He would have liked a show of affection, the *abrazo* that men give each other when they are moved by pride. Instead, everyone in the clan took a step back and eyed him warily.

"But you did start the fire with your eyes. I saw you do it." Tomas leaned against the rail, trying to make the distance between them look casual, not like he was now afraid of his brother after he'd seen his demon in action.

"Yeah, that's one of my tricks." Rafe gazed around the crowd. They'd seen his ugliest form and it had changed the dynamics of the group forever. Of course he'd never planned to take over leadership of the clan, but now there wasn't a chance in hell that these people would accept him in that role.

"Rafael." Marguerite, ballsy woman that she was, actually stepped closer. "We know you did that for Matias. And we appreciate it."

"Yes, Marguerite speaks for all of us. We are headed now to the fueling station to meet Paco. He will take you and the antidote to Santa Cruz. It's too far for you to shift and we think the fastest way to get it there is by speedboat." Miguel wasn't moving any nearer or looking Rafe in the eye either. "I," he cleared his throat. "Well, I don't know how you do what you did, but I'm sure none of us could have handled that witch. You are a hero tonight, Rafael. We won't forget it."

There was a murmur and nods from people in the loose circle that had formed around Rafe. Oh, he believed that.

That they'd never forget this night. He knew his demon was a horrifying reminder of his mother and how she'd stolen his father from the clan. He didn't bother to thank Miguel, just turned when Lacy came up the stairs and straight to his side. The fact that she showed no fear, even put her arms around him, should have shamed the group. Instead, they studied her as if even more suspicious of this were-cat from America. He overheard a whispered question. Could Rafael's woman have demon blood as well?

"How soon until we get to Paco and the boat?" He kept his arm around Lacy.

"Half an hour." Miguel glanced at the sky. "The weather is going to be bad, *amigo*. Maybe you should wait until morning. Paco doesn't want to take you tonight. I talked to him on the radio."

"If he won't take us, we'll use his boat anyway. Grandfather can't wait." Rafe gestured to Ed who stood head and shoulders above the rest of the men. He'd stayed in the back of the crowd. "Eduardo, I seem to remember you are handy on the water. Could you take us to Santa Cruz in Paco's boat? *Will* you?" Ed was one of the few men in the group who didn't seem afraid of him. He appreciated his loyalty and wouldn't forget it.

"Sure." He looked back at the steering station. "Let me check the weather. If a really bad storm is expected, it would be stupid to strike out now."

"Stupid or not, we need to chance it. Grandfather can't afford for us to wait." Rafe looked down when he felt Lacy's elbow in his ribs. "What?"

"I'm going with you." She was deadly serious.

"Not a good idea, sweetheart." Rafe dragged her to the stern where they could have some privacy. "Seriously. You hated your first ride in that little boat. Now, with bad weather sure to dog us, it will be even worse. Are you willing to risk that?"

"Rafe, I'm going." She held onto him.

"If we have trouble, Ed and I can shift out of there and fly on into Santa Cruz. You can't." Rafe hated to play that card, but it was the damned truth. "You'd be a liability. I'd be worried sick about you."

"Give me a life jacket and leave Ed and me on the boat. You can fly in alone with the antidote. Surely you can take it in a pocket or something. I've seen you carry stuff before when you shifted into something small." She had a stubborn tilt to her chin. Rafe wanted to kiss it.

"Yeah, it's in my pocket now, well protected." Rafe patted his cargo pants where he'd stashed it after getting it back from Tomas. "I can take it if I shift, but, baby, you have no idea how horrific the weather can get on the Atlantic. The boat could capsize. You could be thrown into the water."

"So we hang onto the hull and you send out a search and rescue team. Ed will stay with me. I won't drown." Lacy ran her finger down his cheek. "That bitch marked you. She must have had sharp fingernails."

"You have no idea. And you have no idea how crazy you sound right now. That speedboat probably doesn't have a transponder and the Atlantic is huge." Rafe grabbed her hand. "Shit. You're determined, aren't you?"

"You can't leave me here with people who think I might grow horns and speak in tongues any minute." She sighed and hugged him hard. "Yes, I see how they're looking at us. I love a demon. So in their eyes that likely makes me a demon too. Understand?"

"Chica tell you that?" Rafe rested his cheek on her soft hair. Lacy had come on deck looking like a fashion model. She'd even found a dark green t-shirt that made her eyes look like emeralds. If she was going with him, she'd do better to put on one of Ed's shapeless sweatshirts.

"Yes, she's the only one here who seems to like me. But your demon show has everyone here eager to see the last of both of us." Lacy stepped back. "Now are we going together or do I have to swim after the boat until you turn around and pick me up?"

"You're impossible." Rafe kissed her then, he couldn't help himself. "You ready to accept this first?" He dug into one of his deep pockets and pulled out the ring box he had kept with him since that night Lacy had thrown it in his face. It had been in his pocket when Tomas had basically kidnapped him. Now he was glad to have it.

He got down on one knee. "Lacy Devereau, love of my life, mother of my children. You are insane to love me but I can't imagine a better woman to spend the rest of my life with. Will you marry me?" He opened the box and held it out to her.

Lacy teared up. God, how he loved her.

"Yes! I'll even take your name, whatever you decide to call yourself. Castillo, Valdez. I don't care." She snatched the ring and shoved it on her finger, then dragged him to his feet and threw her arms around him. Her kiss said it all.

Rafe was aware of applause and shouts of approval from the crowd. He might not be Mr. Popularity here but love was always a good thing to his people.

"Well now. You have made me very happy." He kissed her ring finger and smiled at Chica who came up to hug Lacy. A few other women edged closer to admire the ring.

Lacy was glowing as she held his hand and accepted best wishes. He was just relieved that this was settled. He wanted to stake his claim on her. He'd spend the rest of his life making sure she didn't regret her decision to take a chance on him.

"Too bad you'll just get your hair wet again on the speedboat. Chica must be a hairdresser in her regular life. You look fantastic." He knew they were getting close to the harbor where Paco was docked.

"She is. She's a genius with a brush and blow dryer. I wish she'd come back to Austin with us, if that's where we end up." Lacy tossed her hair back over her shoulder.

"I do think Austin is where we belong." Rafe glanced toward the part of the deck where the men in the clan had gathered. Tomas was gesturing, still trying to calm them down about his brother the demon. He saw several of them crossing themselves after looking his way. Lacy obviously noticed too.

"Austin. Good. If these people are going to treat you like you're the Anti-Christ, then to hell with them. I sure don't want to raise our children in such a negative environment." She held onto Rafe's hand. "They're going to grow up learning that their father is a hero, facing down evil when he has to. They will certainly never hear a whisper that he could be from the Devil himself." She glared at the gathered shifters. "Ungrateful sods."

"Hmm. Well, thanks." Rafe saw lights in the distance. "Look, we're there. Last chance to change your mind and stay aboard. You and Chica can stay in a cabin and play beauty salon. It'll only take a day, two in bad weather, to get to Santa Cruz on this rig."

"Play beauty salon?" Lacy popped his arm with her fist. "You make me sound like an airhead, Rafe. I'm coming. So grab what you need while I go get that sweatshirt. I know it'll be cold on the water." She raised an eyebrow. "Bet you thought I wouldn't think of that, didn't you?" She turned and ran to the stairs, blowing him a kiss as she disappeared. In a few minutes she was back by his side, obviously determined not to let him out of her sight in case he tried to leave without her.

Rafe realized he was glad she was going. By the time he and Ed had commandeered Paco's boat and made sure they had a full tank, he was on edge and glad of Lacy's warm presence as they struck out across the dark Atlantic in strong winds and a choppy sea. Ed assured them he knew what he was doing and could use the GPS on the boat to get them to Santa Cruz. He revved the motor and they took off, the encouraging shouts of the people on the *No Reglas* ringing in their ears.

No Rules. Too bad that applied to the water and the weather. It kept getting worse, the waves running against them. This was not the night for a fast ride in a small boat. When the rain started, Rafe insisted Lacy stay inside the small cabin while he helped Ed steer against swells as high as skyscrapers. The boat was tossed about and made little headway as driving rain lashed them. They all wore lifejackets now and Ed insisted they tie themselves to the boat when waves kept washing over the gunwales. It was obvious that shifting and trying to fly in the horrible weather conditions would be suicide. They were going to have to wait for it to clear.

When the engine suddenly cut out and then died, Rafe started praying. He could hear Lacy retching down below. Of course she was seasick. He was queasy himself. Even worse, he had no idea where they were or how far from landfall. Shouted questions to Ed didn't get answered. It was impossible to read the instruments in the dark and rain.

When a wall of water came toward them, he and Ed held onto the ship's wheel and each other. Had he killed Shiloh and found the antidote for nothing? Would they all end up at the bottom of the sea? The last thing Rafe heard before he lost consciousness was Lacy screaming his name.

CHAPTER THIRTEEN

Rafe woke up lying in water and staring up at the night sky. The rain had stopped and by some miracle it seemed that the boat had stayed in one piece.

"Rafe?" Lacy crawled out of the cabin. She was drenched and looked scared and shaken.

He untied himself from the wheel, surprised when Ed gave him a hand up. "You okay?" He looked the big man over.

Ed ran his hands down his body and shook his head. "Maybe. Not sure yet. What the hell was that?"

"Have no idea. See if you can get our coordinates. I need to know if we're close enough for me to shift and take the antidote to Grandfather." Rafe helped Lacy to her feet and gathered her into his arms. "Baby, are you hurt?"

"Just banged up a little. God, Rafe, I thought we were facing the end of the world." She clung to him, shivering.

"It was the worst storm I've ever seen out here." He stroked her back. "Let me look at you. You sure you didn't break a bone or hit your head? The way the boat was thrown about in the waves, you must have been--"

"Cats know how to land on their feet. What about you?" She frowned up at him.

"I'm okay, just a little banged up."

She ran her hands over his hair. "You've got a lump the size of a walnut on the back of your head. More than a little banged up I'd say." She kissed his cheek and looked around. "I can't believe it's so calm now. But there's still no land in sight." She pulled him down next to her on the bench seat. "At least I'm over the seasickness. For a while there I was wishing for death."

She wrung out her wet hair and tossed it back over her shoulder. "Have you figured out where we are, Ed? Is it close enough for Rafe to go now?" She looked at Rafe again. "If he's up to shifting."

"I'm up to it. What do you think, Ed?" Rafe kept his arm around Lacy, refusing to give in to the headache that made him want to close his eyes and lean against her.

The giant shifter was hunched over instruments that were obviously waterproof and built to withstand a lot of abuse. He grinned and put his thumb up. "We were lucky. The storm pushed us south, almost on course."

"No kidding." Rafe stood and peered over Ed's shoulder, listening while the shifter gave him specific directions.

"Take off, boss. With the clearing skies, you should be there pretty fast. We'll be right behind you if I can get the engine started." Ed opened a hatch and peered down at a motor swimming in water. "I'll get the pump going even if I have to hand crank it."

"I'll send someone out here after you, no matter what. Give me your exact coordinates." Rafe listened carefully then pulled Lacy up into his arms again. He gave her a hungry kiss, surprised when she clung to him obviously reluctant to let him leave and putting a brave face on it. "Hey now." He brushed her wet hair back and looked up at the clear sky. "Maybe I shouldn't go. Are you going to be all right if I leave you?"

She pasted on a smile which didn't fool him for a minute. "Of course. You've *got* to go now. Save your grandfather. Otherwise what you did to get that antidote was a waste." She touched the wound on his cheek, her smile fading. "Hurry. I don't know how much time we've lost but it seemed like the storm lasted for hours."

Rafe glanced at his waterproof watch and nodded. Yes, it had cost them half the night. If he didn't know better, he'd think Miguel had been right. It was as if there were powers at work, cursing their efforts to save Matias and delaying them at every turn.

"Give me your cell, Lace. Mine's history. What about yours?"

She pulled hers out of a pocket. "This one is definitely ruined. I think I landed on it when I fell off a bunk down there, plus it got wet."

"Okay then. I'll see about replacing both of ours while I'm in Santa Cruz." Rafe stuck it with his in one of his pockets.

"Please. I need to check on the babies as soon as we get a signal." She didn't bother to pretend to be happy to see him going now.

"I'll hurry. I love you. See you soon." One more kiss and Rafe shifted into his strongest bird form, a hawk that had a tremendous wing span. He circled over the boat, which looked damned tiny below him in the vast ocean, then took off. The slight breeze was a tail wind that actually lifted him and made it an easy flight, physically at least. But he was torn between his need to get to his grandfather and worry about leaving Lacy on that boat. She'd sucked it up, but he knew she'd hated being stranded like that.

Before long he saw the many lights of Santa Cruz, a city that never slept, with casinos and a thriving night life. He flew over it, heading for the village that his clan called home. Dark banana plantations rolled beneath him for most of that journey until he came to the scattered lights around the square. The house where his grandfather lay was ablaze. Was that a good sign or bad? He landed and shifted again, running to the door while he dug the padded pouch out of his pocket.

It was a miracle the vials of antidote and poison had survived the storm unbroken. He'd checked before he'd even left the boat. His grandmother met him at the door, her face telling him instantly that he was too late.

"Grandfather?" He wouldn't accept it. He pressed the antidote into her hands.

"Lost his battle an hour ago, Rafael. I'm sorry." She pulled him into her arms and laid her head on his shoulder. "He tried to hold on, sure you were coming to save him. But he was just too weak."

Rafe rested his cheek on her soft hair. Too late. It had all been for nothing. Turning demon, killing that creature. He couldn't regret that but in the end Shiloh had won, damn it. He took a breath that came out too much like a sob. No, strong men didn't cry. He patted his grandmother's back. She soaked his already wet shirt with her tears. Each drop made him feel more like a failure.

"I'm sorry, *Abuela*. I tried..."

"I know you did, *mijo*. You are a good boy." She leaned back and stroked his cheek. "You're wet. Was the crossing rough tonight?"

"More than just rough. We almost lost the boat. I never saw such a storm." Rafe led her to a chair and helped her settle in. "It was as if the witch had put a spell on the weather to torment us."

"You let her live?" His grandmother gripped his hand hard. "I hoped you found that bitch and ended her. Shiloh is the one who did this, isn't she?" For a frail lady, she had strength and could still intimidate him with a stern look. She set the vial on the table in front of her and pointed to it with her other hand. "Answer me, boy. How did you get this? Was it Shiloh who poisoned your grandfather?"

"Yes, she admitted it. She wanted to take over our clan. As Matias's wife. When he refused to set you aside, she made him pay." Rafe looked away from his grandmother's sharp gaze.

"And did you make *her* pay?" She finally let him go.

"Of course I did." He paced the carpet. He couldn't be still, not while he knew Lacy was out there on the water, vulnerable. That freak storm had been no accident of nature. Another storm wasn't out of the question. Shiloh was dead but that didn't mean there weren't others who would like to take over the clan and had the skills to use weather as a weapon.

"How did you make her pay? Answer me, Rafael. Did you kill her?" Grandmother got up to stand beside him. "Please tell me you did."

"Yes, yes I killed her. I ripped off her damned head. Satisfied?" Rafe stopped when she grabbed his arm.

"You did the right thing. Surely you aren't sorry." She shook his arm. "The woman murdered Matias!"

Rafe wouldn't look at her. "I know. But killing isn't easy for me. I did what I had to do but I don't have to like it."

"I'm glad she's burning in hell. Don't let me hear regrets from you again. The bitch needed to be put down." She stepped away from him and swayed on her feet.

"I know that, *Abuela*. But I had to become demon to do it. That takes a toll on me." Rafe ran a hand over his eyes. He hated this, hated the look his grandmother might give him, imagining how he'd done that. Picturing the ugliness of it. To his shock she turned him to face her and put her arms around him.

"My boy. You are what you are. It's no fault of your own. I love you with all my heart. You did something wonderful. It is a blessing you had the power to do the job well." She sighed then kissed his cheek, wiping the moisture from her own cheeks. "Get that look out of your eyes. I am proud of you. I am. But I am also tired. There are many things to do now too. Your grandfather must be laid to rest properly. And a new leader for the clan selected. I, I called your father."

"Emiliano? Why? To lead this clan?" Rafe clenched his fists. "Emiliano has no interest in his family. Hasn't he made that clear by his absence?"

"Your father is my son." Grandmother sat on the couch and pressed a handkerchief to her trembling mouth. "He felt free to stay away because he knew Matias had the clan well in hand." Her shoulders slumped. "Of course Matias could have cared less about the clan after Shiloh got her claws into him, but my son knew nothing of that. Now..." Her voice shook and she gathered herself. "I pray that the shock of losing his father will be what it takes to make Emiliano see where his duty lies. He will come home and take his rightful place here."

"He said he was coming? He is on his way?"

"For the funeral at least." She twisted her handkerchief. "After that we will see."

"How will the others here feel about that? Will they just accept my father as their leader?" Rafe wanted to shake her. But she looked so fragile, so bereft, that he could do nothing but sit beside her and strain for understanding. Was she hoping he would offer to take over the clan himself? Grandmother had always been clever. Was that her end game? For a brief moment Rafe imagined how it would be to put his own stamp on the village. To make sure it became strong again, not as vulnerable to the maneuverings of a demented witch as it was now.

"This is not a democracy, Rafael. This is Clan Castillo. A Castillo will always rule it. Those who do not agree with that are free to leave." She straightened her back, her eyes fierce again. Yes, Grandmother's fire was back and she was going to go her own way, as usual. "Stay and see what happens. If Emiliano won't accept the challenge, then perhaps you will have to step up. It is your birthright."

"Get real, *Abuela*. You were just reminded of what I am. I saw on the ship how the clan feels about demons." Rafe realized he was wasting his breath with that argument. Grandmother had just firmed her lips.

"Listen to me. Be fair. Tomas should lead the clan. He's been here all these years, proving his loyalty. Giving him the chance to lead would be the right thing to do." Rafe laid his hand over hers. "Pushing an unworthy Castillo down people's throats might mean the end of the clan."

"Unworthy? What do you know of your father? He may be the making of the clan." Grandmother was not going to back down.

"I know he ditched his responsibilities here to follow a demon lover around the globe." Rafe got up. "Emiliano won't give her up now either. You are dreaming if you think he's ready to let Lily go and choose the clan. I sure as shit don't have any respect for the man and neither will anyone else here."

"He's coming now. Without her." Grandmother smiled sadly. "He swore it. As for Tomas, he is a fine boy but not a leader. He's not strong like you are, Rafael." She shook her head. "No, my mind is made up. If Emiliano wants it, the clan is his. Now I must rest. Your vampire friends are anxious to leave. Will you speak to them? I have money to pay them." She got slowly to her feet and pulled a pouch out of her pocket. "Euros. I think it is adequate. If not, let me know."

Rafe kissed her cheek and watched her walk wearily up the stairs. When she turned at the top he knew she was going to Grandfather's old room, the master bedroom. How long had it been since she'd slept there? Gossip on the ship said that she'd moved out years ago. Claiming that bedroom might be a sign that she would also consider taking over clan leadership herself if she had to. Rafe sank down on the sofa again, wet clothes and all.

"We saw you talking to your grandmother and didn't want to interrupt." Bart and Caitlin stepped out of the dining room. "I'm sorrier than I can say that I couldn't save your grandfather." The doctor's shoulders sagged.

"I know." Rafe got to his feet and shook Bart's hand. He accepted a hug from Caitlin then gestured to the vial on the table before adding the one still in his pocket. "There's your antidote and the poison too." He explained the significance of the colors. "Take them and analyze the hell out of them. Maybe the knowledge will come in handy someday. I'll know who to call on if something like this happens again."

"Good. If one witch has the formula, it's possible another might as well. You're wise to be ready." Bart held a glass vial up to the light. "I'm sure there's a story behind how you acquired this."

Rafe told them the whole thing, only leaving out the part where Shiloh had been naked when he'd killed her.

"God, she was evil. I'm glad you ended her." Caitlin sat beside him on the sofa and covered his hand. "Is Lacy going to be here soon?"

"I left her stranded in a stalled boat in the Atlantic. I need to grab a boat and go after her. In case they couldn't get the one they're on started. We were in a tremendous storm and our cells are ruined so I can't check on her even if she could get a signal." Rafe rubbed his eyes, struggling to make a mental to do list and failing. "I feel like I haven't slept in weeks."

"Which is why you aren't thinking straight." Bart sat on his other side. "Make a call to Santa Cruz. Send someone else. You don't have to go."

Rafe just looked at him. "Seriously? If Caitlyn were in a similar situation, would you just send someone else?"

"Yes, I'd like to hear your answer to that." Cait stared at Bart, hands on her hips.

"Okay, I get it. Now eat something, Rafe, and I'll arrange for someone to drive you into town if they won't let me do it." Bart jumped up, grabbed Cait and kissed her until she had both hands in his hair. Then he set her away from him and touched her cheek. "No, my love, I would not send someone else if you were stuck afloat in an ocean in a wee boat. I'd move heaven and earth to get to you."

"That's what I wanted to hear. I'll go get Rafe a

sandwich." Cait patted Rafe's shoulder. "Sorry about your grandfather."

"Thanks." Rafe watched Cait rush off toward the kitchen. "You got out of that one well."

"I'm going to marry that woman someday. But she's a stubborn Scot. Hard to pin down." Bart headed for the front door. "Go change into dry clothes while I get you a ride. And make a call, get a boat lined up."

"Right." Rafe rubbed his forehead, willing away a headache from that knock on the head he'd gotten during the storm. Little wonder he wasn't thinking clearly. Grandfather dead. He wanted to wail like a lost child. He hadn't seen Matias in too many years, but always knowing he was out there, a solid rock of reliability, had been a comfort Rafe had subconsciously counted on.

He used the land line to arrange for a boat, then stopped by the room where he was sure his grandfather still lay. He opened the door and stepped inside.

The room was dark but the window had been left open to let fresh air take away the smell of sickness and death. He strode to the bed, stopping next to the slight figure. His grandfather lay as if asleep, his hands on his chest. Someone had dressed him in a dark blue robe. Rafe stretched out his hand to touch silky gray hair. It didn't seem possible that the man who'd always been so alive, so vital was actually gone.

"Thank you, *Abuelo*, for giving me a home." Rafe dashed a hand across his eyes. He didn't have time for this. But his grandfather deserved more than just a moment of mourning. Bending down he touched his forehead to the old man's, whispering the ancient prayer Matias had taught him as a child.

With a sigh, Rafe headed for his room and dry clothes. Lacy was waiting. And his future had to take precedence over his past. There was nothing he could do for his grandfather now except see that the clan was secure before he left the island. He grabbed a quick shower and was feeling almost clear-headed when he got into a speedboat and headed for the position Ed had told him before he'd flown over the Atlantic. Ed had made the radio work and let him know they had drifted off course, south of the old coordinates. It still would be only a matter of half an hour before he should see the boat. A clan member was with Rafe, eager to help tow the boat in since Ed had radioed that the engine was a lost cause.

When the tiny boat finally came in sight, Rafe was happy to see Lacy's red hair blowing in the breeze. She waved, her smile of relief and look of love all he needed to lift his spirits. He had a litany of things going through his head, bringing him down--his clan falling apart, his grandfather dead, even the chance that he'd have to see his father for the first time in centuries. Hell, none of that was as important as keeping the woman he loved safe and by his side. Rafe knew that with Lacy's support, he could get through anything.

CHAPTER FOURTEEN

"Rafe, I'm sorry. Tell me what I can do." Lacy was so glad to be on dry land, she could have danced home. Unfortunately, they weren't going back to Austin just yet. There would be a big funeral for Rafe's grandfather. So far Rafe wasn't saying much about it.

Rafe pulled her across the street, dodging a taxi that swerved to miss them. "Here comes Bart with our new cell phones. The vampires have been great even though the clan's not exactly vamp friendly."

"That's a common attitude with shape-shifters. My cat family isn't crazy about them either. You've heard my mother on the subject." Lacy held on as he towed her down the sidewalk.

"Oh, yeah." Rafe looked exhausted but smiled as Bart and Caitlin approached them. "Santa Cruz has really changed since I was here last. We were lucky they found a cell phone store open at four in the morning."

Bart handed Rafe a package. "We're going to get a hotel room and settle in before dawn. This looks like a nice resort so we've decided to stay a few days and make this a vacation of sorts." He slung his arm around Caitlin. "I hope that doesn't seem ghoulish since I just lost my patient."

"No, I'm glad you're doing that." Rafe handed Lacy her phone.

"Yes, really. Enjoy the island." Lacy hugged both of them goodbye. "Thanks for coming and doing what you could for Rafe's grandfather."

"I wish..." Caitlyn exchanged glances with Bart.

"Say no more. You know this isn't on you." Rafe clearly meant what he said. "Now, I suggest the big white hotel on the end of this avenue. I'll have a suite waiting for you and the clan's paying. Tomas says he makes a fine wine. There will be a case of it for you to take home. If you can't drink it, pass it on to someone who can." He turned to Lacy. "Bart wouldn't accept payment. Can you believe it?"

"That's not right. Let Rafe and the clan do this." Lacy watched Rafe work with his phone. He stepped away and started talking. "Seriously, you guys, the clan can afford it. You should see the yacht I was on yesterday. The old man was loaded. The clan probably owns the big white hotel at the end of the street."

Cait grinned at Bart. "Well, then. We accept graciously. Canary Island wines are legendary."

"I need to thank Rafe." Bart strode over to Rafe.

"Is that an engagement ring on your finger?" Cait grabbed Lacy's hand. "You got your relationship straightened out."

"Yes, I'm going to marry my man. Not sure when but, with our family already started, I'd say it should be sooner rather than later." Lacy turned on her new cell and had a moment when she gulped back tears, sure she'd lost everything. No, it was all there—contacts, pictures, even, uh oh, a dozen missed calls from her mother. She'd given Rafe her passwords and apparently the store had managed to download her information from the Cloud.

"I was going to show you baby pictures, Cait, but my mother is blowing up my phone. God, I hope the babies are all right. She's taking care of them while we're here."

"Call her back, Lacy." Cait grabbed her arm. "I'll give you some privacy." She stepped over to where Bart was still talking to Rafe.

"Yes, sure." Lacy bit her lip as she hit speed dial.

Her mother picked up on the first ring. "Lacy! Thank God! Where the hell have you been?"

"Mama, what's wrong?"

"What's wrong? Didn't you listen to any of my messages? No, of course not. None of my children ever do." Her mother went on a rant then finally took a breath.

"Please, spit it out. Are the babies okay? Is one of them sick? You can call Ian you know."

"The children are fine. So far. But I am not. I'm about to have a nervous breakdown. And I will not go to that vampire doctor. You can trust me on that. Blood sucking creep. I swear he hit on me. Patted my bottom when you were in labor."

Lacy began to think this was no big deal. Her mother was still a beautiful woman and single. Did she have a thing for Ian? How funny that would be. But all those messages...

"Why the nervous breakdown? Get to the freaking point, Mama."

"Okay, here it is. Why the hell didn't you tell me that your Rafe is a demon?" Her mother sounded breathless. Or was that sobbing?

"Wait a minute. How do you know that?" Lacy gripped the phone.

"I don't hear a denial, do I?" No sobs. That was anger. "Lacy, how long have you known this?"

"Mama, that doesn't matter. Now answer me. Who has been filling your head with such talk?" Lacy glanced at Rafe. He, Bart and Cait were laughing about something a few feet away. Good for them. While she was here dealing with a hysterical mother.

"Who has been talking to me? Seems there was a woman at my door this week, claiming to be Rafe's mother. What a surprise. At first I think, okay, the children will have another grandmother, a shape-shifter of course. But then I really look at her." Mama took a deep breath and blew it into the phone.

"She's not a regular shifter. Oh, no. She's beautiful, Lacy. Cold as ice and so evil my back teeth hurt. Evil! Like she came straight from hell! I'm thinking of going back to church just to be on the safe side. Could she have taken my soul and I don't know it yet?" Yep, that was a sob this time.

"Now, Mama, this sounds crazy. No one can just steal your soul. I think," Lacy looked around frantically for Rafe. What did she know about demons? He had his back turned to her as he pointed down the street and said something to Bart. "I think you have to make a deal. Sell your soul or trade something."

"You are not making me feel better. Besides, you weren't here, Lacy. You didn't see her." Her mother was on a roll now. "Her name is Lily. She looks nothing like Rafe. She's blond and blue eyed. But it's an unnatural blue. Then, when she stares at you, her eyes glow red. Red, Lacy! I'm so scared of her I wet myself. Yes, you heard me. I pissed my panties." Noisy sobs went on for much too long.

"Mama, calm down. Maybe she's not really Rafe's mother. It could be an imposter. What proof did she have? Come on now. Listen to me."

"Imposter? I wish. But she had a picture. Of a family. It was her, Rafe's father who is the image of him and her holding a baby Rafe. She claimed that was her proof."

"Mama, Rafe's a thousand years old. They didn't have photos back then."

"Well! Maybe she lied to me. But I believed her anyway, about being his mother. She knew things. About his clan. Where you and he are right now."

"Is she still there?" Lacy was pretty sure she couldn't be if her mother was able to call. Unless this person wanted to get Rafe there, back in Austin. Demons were tricky. She'd seen that firsthand when Glory had dealt with them.

"No, she stayed so long I was terrified I'd have to offer her dinner. I was positively starving. You know how I get if my blood sugar gets too low."

"Focus, Mama." Lacy knew a discussion of her mother's blood sugar and dietary needs could last a half an hour. "Maybe you've seen the last of her."

"I wish. But she'll be back. That's what she said. Like the Terminator or something. You should have heard her. As if she was talking from the bowels of Hell itself." Her mother sniffled.

Lacy frowned and finally got Rafe's attention. He hurried to her side. The bowels of hell? If her mother only knew.

"Listen to me, Daughter. You have to come home right this minute. If this is Rafe's mother, I don't know what to do. Should I grab the babies and run? Where can we go? And what will I do if she tries to take them away from me?"

"Mama, stay put. Let me think." Think? Lacy was trying not to throw up. She slid down to land on the concrete. Rafe sat next to her.

"Lacy! What the hell?" Rafe slid his arm around her. "Bad news? Our children? What?"

She waved at him to shut up. "What did you do when Lily showed up, Mama? Did you let her see the babies, hold them?" Lacy saw Rafe's face pale. Yes, he knew who Lily was and was just as horrified as she was. Not reassuring. "Mama!"

"I couldn't stop her! She walked right past me as if I was invisible. I tried to get between her and the little ones and she just shoved me aside like I was nothing." Gulping sobs now. "She's so powerful! I couldn't protect them, Lacy!"

"No, I'm sure you tried your best. Please stop crying." Lacy wiped her own eyes with one hand.

"You've got to come home, Lacy. Bring Rafe. Maybe he can get rid of her. He has to! She swore he was a demon too. Is he?" She gulped.

"Let's not get into that on the phone. Tell me more, Mama." Lacy gripped Rafe's hand. "How was she with the babies?"

"You should have seen her, Lacy. She stared down at the babies with those red eyes of hers for the longest time. I'm afraid, uh, afraid she put some kind of evil demon spell on them."

"Why would she do that? If they're her grandchildren, Mama? She'll, uh, she'll love them." Lacy looked at Rafe. "Won't she?"

He shook his head and took the phone.

"I'm sorry, Sheila. I had no idea my mother even knew about the children. And Lily is my mother. I'll handle her. Please do your best to hang in there. We'll be home as soon as we can." Rafe put his arm around Lacy.

Lacy couldn't help it, she flinched.

"Here's Lacy." He shook his head and got up. "I'm going to call and make sure the clan's plane is ready to go. After what I did for them, they owe me that."

"Mama, Rafe's arranging transportation. We're coming." What could she say to make her mother calm down? Nothing. Because she was freaking out too. "Listen. Things are bad here. Rafe's grandfather died. We may have to come back to bury him. His clan may need Rafe. I should..." She couldn't finish the thought.

"Your children need you. They come first. Tell him that. His mother," Her own mother howled, yes, gave a full throated cat howl of distress. "Is too dangerous to be allowed near these children again. I can't deal with this alone. If Rafe loves his children, he needs to be here to protect them."

"I get that. He understands it too. He's doing the right thing. I'm sorry you're having to deal with this. But you are doing all you can. We'll be there as soon as possible. I'll call you back when I know more." Lacy ended the call then looked up when Rafe walked back to her side. Cait and Bart apparently had enough vampire hearing to know what was what.

"You need us for anything, call." Bart was solemn and kept his arm around Caitlyn.

"Thanks." Rafe helped Lacy to her feet. "Will do. But I think we can handle things from here. Enjoy your vacation. You've earned it."

The vampires nodded then headed down the street. Nice to have understanding friends.

Rafe kept his hands on Lacy's shoulders. Good thing because she was feeling wobbly as hell.

"The plane has gone to pick up my father. Apparently he was in London. It will be back here later today. We can leave then. It's the fastest way to get home." Rafe looked into her eyes and then must have decided she was fine with it and pulled Lacy close, running his hand over her back. "You okay?"

"What do you think? My mother said Lily was staring at the babies with red eyes." Lacy took a deep breath. Sea air and car exhaust. Ugh. Her stomach heaved. She stepped back. "What does that mean, Rafe?"

"Damned if I know. But we're going to find out." Rafe steered her toward a jeep nearby. "I'm sorry. But I can't imagine she would hurt them. She's probably just satisfying her curiosity. She sure as shit never bothered with me."

"What about the clan? Your grandfather's funeral?"

"I've done what I could. Grandmother's not going to be happy when we take off this quickly but she should understand that I have to protect my children." He slammed the car door. "It's better if I leave now anyway. I have nothing to say to my father. I'm just surprised Lily is in Austin without him. I'm not sure what that means."

Lacy leaned against him. Despite the fact that he was saying nothing, she knew the signs: jaw so clenched it could have been cut from granite and eyes firmly fixed on the windshield as he stabbed the key into the ignition. Rafe was upset and about to lose it. And no wonder. His grandfather had just died and now he was going to have to cope with parents who'd never given a rat's ass about him. He looked like he wanted to either howl at the sliver of moon sinking in the sea nearby or slam his fist into something.

"I'm sorry we're going to miss the funeral. Are clan funerals a big deal?"

"They can be. Especially for the leader." Rafe started the car. "Forget it. No one would want me there anyway."

"Screw those ungrateful bastards. You got justice for him." She could see nothing she was saying was helping. He was driving too fast for these mountain roads. She was glad for her seatbelt but knew better than to tell him to slow down. "At least you got to see your grandfather before he died, Rafe. Maybe it was just his time to go."

"We're immortal, Lacy. We're not supposed to have a 'time'." His voice was rough and if Lacy didn't know better, she'd think he was on the verge of tears.

"Pull over. Stop the jeep and pull over."

"Are you sick?" He did as she asked though.

When the jeep shuddered to a stop, Lacy grabbed his ears and turned his head so she could look into his eyes. "It's not weak to want to grieve for a man who was like a father to you, you know." She saw him glance around. "No one's here. No one's looking, macho man. And you don't have to cry buckets if that's not in you." She kissed him gently. "But later, when we're on the plane with nothing but time, tell me about Matias. All the things he did for you when you were young. Stories about him. Okay?"

"Yeah, I'd like that." Rafe leaned his cheek against her hair and put his arms around her. "He was like a father to me. I loved him. He accepted me. As his blood." He blinked and looked away. "But it's the demon blood we have to worry about now. My mother is at best unpredictable. I'm sick that she's taken an interest in the children. If one of them shows signs of having some demonic powers…" He put the car into gear and hit the road again, at a reasonable speed this time. "Well, we may never get rid of her."

"But you have powers and she didn't pay attention to you." Lacy realized she was gnawing off her thumbnail. Not good for a cat to dull her claws.

"That's because Matias had enough clout to keep her away from me." Rafe sped up again. "He gave up on my father, exchanging my dad for me. Lily understood that it was in her own interests to just let Grandfather have me and move on. She had a passion for my father that came first for her. And I don't think she ever realized just how powerful I'd grow up to be." He shrugged. "If she could have seen me against Shiloh, she would have been proud." His knuckles were white on the steering wheel. "Proud as hell."

"Rafe, quit beating yourself up over killing her. I'm glad you have a conscience but you did the right thing." Lacy laid her hand on his arm.

"Murder is never the right thing." He glanced at Lacy, his mouth in a grim smile. "Yes, I can rationalize it, but I won't let it go and I won't forget it. It sickened me." He finally took one hand off the wheel and gripped hers. "You don't know what your love means to me, Lace. I wouldn't blame you if you decided I wasn't worth it. I come with way too much baggage."

"Who doesn't?" But as she held onto his hand, Lacy wondered if she wasn't a little insane to just accept a man with a demon mother hovering over her babies. Too late for regrets now. She'd had his children. One or more of them… "Any chance we could have spawned a little demon, Rafe?"

"Here we go again." He dropped her hand as he wheeled into the village and parked in front of his grandfather's house. "Lily will be glad to tell us the answer,

I'm sure. And, for the record, I hate that word 'spawned.' It makes us seem less than human." He cut the engine. "But maybe that's how you see me now."

"Rafe, no!" Lacy had known the minute she'd said it that it was the wrong word.

He turned to Lacy, his dark eyes suddenly glowing red "This, this is what you look for in a demon child. It's what sent my clansmen running away screaming when I was a kid. You want to call your mom and tell her to check our children for that?" He let the glow die away and waited.

Lacy swallowed and pressed her hand to her stomach. "No, I don't think so. When we get home will be soon enough to share that little helpful hint." She grabbed the door handle. "I am going to be sick." She stumbled out of the jeep and ran to the house just as his grandmother came outside. The lady gave her a pitying look but Lacy ignored it and headed straight for the first bathroom she found. She fell to the floor in front of the toilet and succumbed to dry heaves. Seasickness had left her empty. When Rafe found her there, he said nothing, just wiped her face with a cool cloth and sat beside her until she fell against him.

"I love you. Whatever you decide, please remember that." His voice was rough as he rubbed her back.

"Decide? We have a family, Rafe. The decision was made over nine months ago. When we had unprotected sex." Lacy closed her eyes. "I don't regret the children. I'll never regret them. Do I know what I would have done if I'd known about the demon blood you carry back then? No idea. But I love you and I want to be with you. That hasn't changed. I still think you are a fine man and will be a great father. As long as you can keep your demon relatives away, we won't have a problem."

He sighed and she felt his chest move behind her. "What did I ever do to deserve you?"

"Shut up." Lacy turned in his arms. "You are my man. You deserve everything, never doubt it." She rubbed her cheek against his scruff. "If my mouth didn't taste like pond scum, I'd kiss you senseless. Wait a minute." She jumped up, turned on the water in the sink behind her and scrubbed her mouth out with a wet washcloth. "There, that's better."

Rafe grinned and stood next to her. "You didn't have to do that on my account. I could have gone for some pond scum." He pulled her in and took her mouth hungrily, lips, teeth, tongue, as if he'd never get enough.

Lacy finally eased back. "You're crazy. You do realize my stomach is still gurgling, don't you?"

"I can hear it. It's scaring me to death or I'd still be kissing you." Rafe pulled her to the door. "Let me see what I can do about that."

"Is there such a thing as a Coke in this village?" Lacy snuggled against him. "That should help."

"You've got it. And how about a shower? I know you have to be itching from that salt water bath you took on the boat."

"God, yes, a shower." Lacy looked up and traced the new lines between his eyebrows that had seemed to appear overnight. "Join me and I may actually be on my way to recovery."

"I'd like nothing better." He opened the bathroom door and called a name. "Come with me. I'll show you to our room." He said something in Spanish to the servant who'd appeared, then he led Lacy up the stairs. They had a suite of rooms with an attached bath. Before Lacy could strip off her sticky clothes, the woman arrived with a bottle of soda and a glass of ice. Once the door was closed and locked, Rafe made quick work of stripping her down. Lacy gulped the cold liquid then stepped into the shower which he'd started at the perfect temperature.

"Are you coming in?" Lacy held out her hand. A knock on the hall door got Rafe's attention.

"Just a minute." Rafe stalked over to the door. A whispered conversation started to get loud.

"Take care of your clan business, Rafe. I'm going to get

clean then lie down for a nap." Lacy watched him disappear into the hall, then washed off quickly, wrapping herself in a robe hanging on a hook behind the door.

A nap? As if she could sleep with this whole demon thing to process. His mother was threatening her children. Oh, not to hurt them but what if she wanted to take one as a protégé? The idea didn't bear thinking about. Lacy closed her eyes and tried to imagine Rafe's mother. Beautiful and cold. Her own mother was beautiful but warm and full of fire. The two going head to head would be quite a sight. But a demon and were-cat? It was a mismatch. Hell was bound to be the winner.

Lacy succumbed to exhaustion brought on by the resent stress of childbirth and being tossed about in a tiny boat in the Atlantic. Oh, and then there was the jet lag because she'd flown from Austin to the Canary Islands too. No wonder she couldn't keep her eyes open. It was almost a relief to let her mind go blank and sink into sleep and nightmares.

CHAPTER FIFTEEN

They were at the airport early. When the plane landed, the man who got off was a stranger, but Rafe knew this was the father who'd left him all those years ago. The crew got busy refueling and taking on a new pilot for the long flight to Austin.

"Rafael." Emiliano held out his hand. Rafe ignored it. "Where are you going? Your grandfather isn't in the ground yet. Where is your respect?"

"Are you really going to lecture me? Where were you when he was dying?" Rafe turned his back to pull their bags out of the jeep and hand them to Ed who was flying back with them. "Lacy, why don't you get on the plane? I know you're exhausted. The bed in the back cabin is comfortable. You don't have to wait for take-off to settle in."

"Good idea. I'll look it over." Lacy followed his lead and ignored his father, walking past the man to climb the steps into the sleek plane with the fancy gold "C" on the side. "Are you coming?"

"In a minute. My father wants to talk. Maybe it's time." He nodded to Ed. "Can you make sure the plane is ready to go as soon as possible?"

"You got it, boss." Ed hurried away to confer with the ground crew.

"You should stay. What does your grandmother say about your leaving now?" Emiliano nodded toward the black limo waiting a few yards away. He was getting first class treatment. "Change your mind. Show a united front to the clan. The family needs to remain close at a time like this."

"Remain close? When have we ever been close?" Rafe looked his father up and down. He could have been looking in a mirror, except that Emiliano hadn't bothered to stay in shape. He looked soft. A shifter didn't stay frozen in time like vampires did. Muscles came through workouts. Rafe had always made it his business to be in top form and ready to defend himself. He'd worked as a bodyguard for years because of that.

Emiliano had obviously been more concerned with his wardrobe, tonight a black suit tailored in London, and his hair, cut by a gifted stylist. He'd defend himself with a checkbook, not his fists. He'd probably used Lily and her credit line for financial support. Rafe didn't want to think about where that money came from.

"Where is Lily? I thought you two were joined at the hip. Now I hear she's in Austin and you're here without her." Rafe forced his fists to relax by his sides.

"We are done. I don't want to discuss your mother." Emiliano looked around the airport. "This place is unrecognizable. So much change."

"Yes. But wait until you see clan headquarters. I'm afraid it won't meet your high standards." Rafe realized he was tense again and breathed. "Seriously? After a thousand years you and Lily just called it quits? I don't believe you. You gave up everything for her. Even your own son."

"You sound bitter, Rafael. Haven't you ever been in love?" Emiliano brushed an invisible speck off his jacket. "But then what I had with Lily wasn't love, was it? With a demon you are not in love, you are ensorcelled. She finally freed me." He nodded. "So here I am."

"Good timing. You can take Grandfather's place." Rafe didn't believe a word out of his father's mouth.

Emiliano smiled. "Yes. It will be my pleasure. Santa Cruz looks prosperous. I'm sure the clan is doing well, despite what the home place may look like."

"Yes, there's money. Don't spend it all too fast, Father, on your wardrobe." Rafe walked toward the plane which had started warming up its engines.

"Wait. You could stay. Help me with the clan businesses. Your grandmother tells me you have been running a successful one in America."

Rafe turned, not sure he'd heard correctly. "Seriously? You want my help? Why the hell would I do that? You never sent me as much as a post card in all the years you've been gone. You claim you were under a spell? I don't believe you. I think you were your father's son, so busy chasing tail that you had no time for anything else. You're just lucky it hasn't killed you like it did Matias."

"That's enough!" His father raised his hand then saw something in Rafe's face that made him fail to follow through.

Rafe knew what Emiliano had seen, he'd let his eyes go red. "What's the matter, Father? Afraid of your demon child?" He laughed. "Yeah, I have the goods your woman passed on to me and I know how to use them. You *should* be afraid. I wouldn't advise hitting me. It might be your last act on Earth."

"You threaten your own father? Of course you would be unnatural. You aren't human, are you?" Emiliano drew himself up, trying to look powerful. It didn't work.

It took everything in Rafe not to pop out his horns then and there. Not human? Oh, he'd like to do a demo that would blow his father's mind. "I am what you and Lily made me. Matias was the only father I ever knew and he's gone now so I'm leaving." Rafe gestured toward the plane. "I'm going home and that home isn't here, that's for damn sure. I have a family now that means something to me. The clan doesn't. You guaranteed that when you walked away from me centuries ago. I learned the hard way that it's easy to forget clan ties."

"Go. I'm done with demons. You were a mistake I've always regretted. Mother told me you couldn't even save your grandfather with all your so-called powers and Matias loved you, more fool him. You will not be missed at his funeral. In fact, the clan will be glad to have seen the last of you." Emiliano turned and stalked toward the waiting car.

Rafe watched him go and damned himself for ever talking to the son of a bitch. What had he expected? That Emiliano would regret abandoning him as a baby? Even ask his forgiveness? His selfish father never regretted anything except fathering a half-demon child. And now he'd lead the clan, probably run it into the ground indulging his expensive tastes. But forget all that. Rafe was no longer interested in the clan. Not at all.

He looked toward the plane and saw Lacy standing in the doorway. She held out her hand, beckoning him to join her. Had she heard his father's cold dismissal? If she had, she never mentioned it as she pulled him into a seat, handed him a cold drink and then called her mother to tell her they were on the way home. Her hand was in his when they took off smoothly. After they were airborne, she invited him to the large double bed in the back cabin and seduced him.

Making love with Lacy went a long way toward convincing Rafe that he was not a piece of trash that his parents had discarded so they could wander the world in search of their own pleasure. She loved him and proved it with her clever hands and mouth. Rafe groaned when she pulled him on top of her and begged him to take her. She scored his back with her claws, purring in his ear with satisfaction. Before they were through he rolled her so that she rode him. He carefully grasped her plump breasts and held on, loving the way her eyes closed and she bit her lip when she came.

How could he be worthless when such a woman believed in him, loved him and trusted him enough to have his children? He pulled her down by his side and stroked her hip. God, he may not deserve her, but he had her and he was going to keep her. She'd be safe with him and his children would be too or he'd die protecting them. Die? No, he'd live and be around for a long, long time. Somehow he'd make sure of it. Sleep claimed him on that thought.

They landed in Austin on a sunny day, a half a world away from his clan and Grandfather's funeral. Rafe put that sad event out of his mind as he helped Lacy into his SUV. A phone call had made it possible to get one of his employees from the club to bring the car to the airport. Ed was being picked up by a friend and waved before taking off. Rafe knew he owed the man a big bonus for coming to Santa Cruz and helping out. He'd see to it if his club hadn't gone into the crapper while he'd been gone.

But forget business, he had much more important things to worry about now. He drove toward Lacy's mother's house while she used her cell to check in. Her tense smile wasn't reassuring.

"Yes, we just landed and we're on our way. Is she there now?" Lacy squeezed Rafe's thigh. "Good. We'll grab the kids and go. Did Lily leave a phone number where she can be reached? I don't want her showing up and bothering you again."

"Okay. I'll have Rafe call her and let her know our plans. Thanks, Mama. See you in a few minutes." Lacy ended the call then turned to him and sighed deeply. "She isn't there now. Mama is packing up everything so we can grab the babies and take them home."

"She got Lily's phone number?" Rafe wished he had time to think. "I want to warn her to stay away from

Sheila. Like you said." But he hadn't spoken to his mother in centuries. He had a headache again and couldn't blame it on that lump on his head this time. That had subsided. No, this was dread. Lacy got sick to her stomach when she was stressed. He got blinding headaches and this one was coming on strong.

"She's texting it to me." Lacy's phone chimed. "Here it is. Maybe you should pull over and call her now, Rafe. I don't want her to be there when we drive up."

"You think if I call her and order her to do something she'll just say, okey dokey?" Rafe knew sarcasm wasn't the way to go here but he was close to losing it. Fuck. He should have had a vasectomy centuries ago. Though he doubted they did such a procedure back then, not without a mallet for a nut cracker.

He didn't regret having children. He loved each one of them but so far he'd just seen their pictures. He couldn't wait to hold them. The girl, Daniela, was the image of Lacy, already his little princess. And the boys... He could imagine doing the Little League thing, all the sports he'd wished they'd had when he was a kid. Normal stuff. He'd even coach if he could watch enough videos on the Internet to learn the rules and the skills for whatever sports the boys wanted to play. Before they were born he'd started making plans, bought a couple of balls, and looked at some houses with basketball goals and big yards...

Some would say those were foolish dreams when a man is half demon. He should have known hell would come calling eventually and want its piece of his soul. But he wasn't going to let that happen. He'd finally come to terms with his demon side and, by damn, he was going to learn to accept it and use it to his advantage. He was strong, he knew he was a good man and no demon was going to get the better of him, not even his own mother.

No one, not even Lucifer himself, was going to take away his children's happiness. He'd make sure of it. He pulled into a convenience store parking lot and dug his

153

phone out of his pocket.

"Tell me her number. I have to make this call from my cell. I don't want her to have access to yours." He grimly put the digits into his phone and listened to ringing. When her voice came on, he almost couldn't talk, but finally made himself speak. "Lily, this is Rafael."

"I expected I'd hear from you, son. How proud you must be of your children. The boys, so sturdy and looking just like you. And the girl... I can see she will break many hearts as she grows to maturity. Lovely." Her laugh was merry.

"Stay away from my children." That came out a growl.

"Now is that any way to talk to your mother? I have discovered I quite like being a grandmother. It is fascinating to see the gene pool ripple forth. Don't you think?" She hummed.

"I think you have no right to call yourself a mother. You left me without a backward glance centuries ago. It is much too late to claim a kinship now. You will never have a relationship with any of my kids." Rafe felt the plastic case crack in his hands and eased up. God, but he hated her. She sounded so smooth, so sure of herself. While he was on the edge of an explosion that could make the car shake. If he turned demon here and now what would Lacy think? Do? He couldn't. She loved him and trusted him but the less she saw of his demon side the better. Even he didn't like to look in a mirror when he had his demon on.

"Look out your car window." Lily was suddenly serious. "Come. We need to speak privately. Without your little cat twitching her ears. We must meet face to face."

Rafe saw his mother a few feet away, beside the store at the edge of a wooded area. "Fine." He turned off the phone and tossed it into Lacy's lap. "I'll be right back."

She looked past him and her eyes widened. "Is that--?"

"My demon mother? Yes. She wants to discuss things. I'm going to set her straight about our children." Rafe unbuckled his seatbelt and opened the car door. "Stay here, lock yourself in. If I'm not back in fifteen minutes, go on to your mother's. I'll see you at home at our place later. This may take a while. Lily and I have a lot of history to discuss."

"Be careful. She's powerful, you said." Lacy reached out for him and he stopped long enough to drop a kiss on her lips.

"So am I, babe, so am I. Don't worry. What is it Lily told your mother?" He deliberately lowered his voice. "I'll be back." Then he grinned and climbed out of the car. He walked over to where his mother had disappeared into the woods. Good idea. If things headed south and they both went demon, they didn't need an audience.

"Look at you, so strong, so sure of yourself." Lily stepped out from behind a tree. "I heard how you handled that witch Shiloh. Impressive."

"Somehow I knew you'd like that. Do you have spies everywhere? Or was Shiloh working for you? You never did like Matias." Rafe crossed his arms over his chest and leaned against a tree trunk.

"No, I hated him. Matias laid down the law and I let him bully us. Foolish of me. I never should have chosen your father instead of you. What was I thinking?" She threw up her hands. "Emiliano. One phone call from his mommy and he decides to go back to the clan. Claims I had him under a spell. As if I'd bother." She blinked her long lashes, her eyes bright with unshed tears.

"Yes, he told me that story." Rafe was fascinated by her. Was this her power? This mesmerizing speech and look that men couldn't look away from?

"We were together because we wanted to be. He has a taste for what I can give him." She laughed. "I won't say what it is. But I don't doubt he'll come crawling back once he bleeds his clan dry. The man is very expensive. I won't have him though. I will laugh in his handsome face." She opened and closed her hands, as if struggling for control.

"It's what he deserves, I'm sure." Rafe almost felt sorry

for her. He couldn't believe it.

"Never mind. I know now he was a mistake. I let his charm blind me to his weaknesses. He is not strong like you are, Rafael. But then he doesn't carry my blood." Her cold smile made Rafe shiver.

"Did you arrange for Shiloh to kill my grandfather?" Rafe took a step toward her.

She shook her head. "Why would I work with a low level witch? It is beneath me. If I wanted Matias dead, I've have killed him a thousand years ago and taken you with me. Instead I listened to Emiliano and left with him. Left you and your precious grandfather in that backwater town to do as you pleased. Too bad that you were not appreciated there."

She sighed. "Stupid peasants. They did not realize that demon blood is to be celebrated. Look at how you used it to get revenge for Matias!" She paced the forest floor. "There should have been a parade, fireworks. You should have been honored and made leader of the clan. Instead, they bring back Emiliano?" She spit on the leaves beneath her feet. "Pah! He has done nothing to deserve the honor of heading the clan. He will have the title, the riches and you, our son, get the bum's rush out of town."

"Save the fake maternal rant. You're a thousand years too late. I wanted to leave. But, thanks to you scaring Lacy's mother and looming over my children like a vulture from hell, I couldn't even stay for Grandfather's funeral." Rafe held his ground when her eyes glowed red, even though a wise man would have run for his life. "What the fuck do you want with my kids?"

"Obviously Matias didn't teach you respect for your elders." She sniffed but her eyes settled into blue again. "I had to see them, Rafael. I wanted to know if our blood runs true. You will see for yourself. They have much of your shifter clan in them. Much of the cat. But there is one, Rafael, one who shows great promise. I will let you see for yourself as time passes." She laughed and moved toward him. "Did you think I came here to take one of them? Drag one of them down to hell with me?"

"Why wouldn't I? Maybe you've finally discovered some maternal feeling in that withered breast of yours." Rafe knew it was a low blow. Withered she was not. She was stunning, forever in her prime. Her golden hair was shining and her lips were the kind men dreamed of kissing. She had a figure that would make a centerfold jealous. She showed it off in a snug blue dress the color of her eyes. He could analyze her without lust but most men would be hard just glancing at her. Seduction was her talent and he was sure she used sex to drag men to hell with her so she could steal their souls.

His father had been an easy mark. As she'd said, he was weak. Just like his grandfather had been about women. It was why it had taken Rafe so long to commit to one woman for life. He'd seen too much of what happened when a man is led by his cock.

She was suddenly right in front of him and paralyzed him with a touch to his cheek. "My boy. You lash out because I hurt you so. Yet you are grateful, aren't you, that I didn't take you with me to train you in demon ways? You could have been a great demon. Lucifer has mocked me for giving you up. For letting you be a mere shifter instead of what should have been your destiny. I have been punished for letting you slip through our fingers. Did you know that?"

Rafe couldn't move away from her hand, warm on his face, but he could speak. "No, I didn't know that. Why abandon me? I, I wanted parents. A real home."

She slapped him then, so hard his head snapped back. "Stupid boy. I gave you loving grandparents, a real home. Not my fault the other children didn't understand what you were and love you as you deserved. What do you think your life would have been like with Emiliano and me? In Hell half the year? He will never speak of it because I wiped his memory each time we left there, but it is torture, pain, humiliation. You would have seen it, remembered it and learned from it. Because that is what demons do to grow to their full potential." She kissed the spot where she'd hit him.

"Oh, hold onto your anger and your hurt, I don't care. I have no human feelings. But remember this as you raise your children: I am letting you keep them. Lucifer would like nothing better than for me to claim the one who shows promise now. But I am going to go down there and lie my pretty ass off. It is good that he still finds me beautiful and charming. He will choose to believe me when I say the child is not worth it. The powers weak and not worth the fight it would cause with you and the friends you have made here on Earth." She whirled away, her blue skirt swishing around her legs.

"You would do that? For me?" Rafe couldn't believe it could be that easy.

"Everything I've done has been for you, dear boy. Believe me or not. Of course it won't be easy. For me." She waved a hand and vanished. Before Rafe could react, she shimmered into sight again. "And by the way? If you want to know who was behind Shiloh's attack on your grandfather? Think. Who hated Matias more than anyone else? Who is there now, happy to be rid of him and eager to be the power behind the throne? Eh?" And, having sown the seeds of Rafe's misery to her satisfaction, she smiled and disappeared again.

Rafe staggered, then sat on the ground and went over the conversation in his mind a half dozen times. When he came up with the answer to his mother's last riddle, he bowed his head to his knees. Grandmother. Surely not. But who else? She had her son back and control of the clan through him. And she'd rid herself of a faithless husband.

When he heard the crunch of leaves behind him, Rafe turned, thinking maybe Lily had come back to laugh at him. Of course she wanted one of the babies after all.

How could she give up a chance to have a demon child a second time? He sagged in relief when he saw Lacy, holding a tire iron and looking scared half to death.

"Really? You going to hit a demon with that?" Rafe got up and took it out of her shaking hands. "Lily would have used some kind of power that would have ended up with you wearing it through your large intestine."

"God, Rafe, do you have to be so graphic?" She sagged against him, wrapping her arms around his waist.

"Just telling it like it is." He breathed in her clean fragrance then dropped a kiss on top of head. He looked around and inhaled again. No sign or scent of demon. So Lily had really left.

"Where is she? Do I need to call my mother to tell her to get out the crosses and holy water?" Lacy pulled her cell out of her pocket.

"No, Lily's gone and won't be back. Pretty sure of that anyway." Rafe started walking back toward the car. "And hold the holy water. It gives me the willies." He kept his arm around her until she was in the car. "Let's go pick up our children. Didn't you tell me Ian patted your mother's butt? You think there could be something going on there?"

"Between Ian and my mom?" Lacy looked at him like he was crazy. "I don't know. Wait a minute. Lily's just gone? You talked her out of doing anything with the babies? She's no threat now?"

"That's right. She's off to talk to Lucifer. She's claiming the kids are off limits to demons and will stay that way." Rafe decided that was all Lacy needed to know for now. "I meant to ask her about that photo she showed your mom. That was quite a trick."

"I guess demons can fake anything. But that's great news, Rafe. And you're okay with letting the clan go?" She climbed back into the SUV.

Rafe stuck the tire iron into the back of the car then got into the driver's seat. "I let the clan go centuries ago, Lace. This was a reminder that it was best for me to move on.

My father needs to step up and take his rightful place there. He may have some trouble getting people to follow him after being away so long, but that's his problem. My grandmother will make sure everyone falls in line. Lily says she and Emiliano are done and I believe her. So that will help. Emiliano without demon baggage will be easier for the clan to stomach. If Lily had my father under some kind of spell all these years, she must have removed it. She claims she didn't, but who knows?"

"Well then." Lacy sat back, finally looking relaxed. "So you and your mother cleared the air."

"You could say that. She explained some things I always wondered about. I needed to hear what she had to say. I will never call her Mother and we won't invite her for Christmas dinner, but I feel better about my history than I have for a long time." Rafe realized that was true. Huh. They *had* cleared the air. Too bad it had taken so long. When he thought about a life spent in Hell, he shuddered. Yes, being left with the clan had been the best thing for sure. Grandmother and Grandfather had loved him and done what they could for him. Looking back, he could see that now.

By the time he and Lacy got to the were-cat enclave, Sheila had three baby car seats on her porch and a ton of baby stuff ready to go. Lacy jumped out of the SUV and hugged her mother, filling her in on the news.

"You sure I won't have to be looking over my shoulder for years to come in case a demon wants one of these children?" Sheila had announced that it was feeding time and they'd just finished giving the three babies a bottle. Now she stood over the bassinets she'd set up in her spare bedroom. She'd decorated the space in green, her compromise color as she called it, and announced that she'd be happy to babysit when Rafe and Lacy went on their honeymoon. Rafe took the hint.

"She's gone, she swore it. I think we'd better set a wedding date, babe. Your mother is ready to marry you off." He was playing with son number one's toes, checking his eyes surreptitiously. Lucas did look like him, dark eyes and dark fuzz on his head.

"How about Valentine's Day?" Lacy held their daughter, patting her lightly on the back until she burped. "I think that would be romantic."

"Sounds good to me. Will that give you time to get everything together, Sheila?" Rafe asked his soon to be mother-in-law the question since he knew she was the one who wanted to throw a cat-style shindig at the enclave. Son number two, Gabriel, blinked up at him sleepily when Rafe rubbed his tummy. Golden eyes, same dark fuzz. No sign of red eyes. Rafe wanted to sigh in relief.

"Sure. We can do it. Lacy's been planning her dream wedding since she was a little girl, haven't you, sweetheart?" Sheila laughed when Lacy flushed.

"Mom! You're embarrassing me." Lacy handed their daughter, who'd decided to fuss, to Rafe. "See if you have the magic touch. I don't know what she wants. She's been fed and changed."

Rafe handled her gingerly, while she wailed her displeasure. "Do you have a dream wedding, Lacy?"

"Maybe. Every little girl does." She leaned over to kiss Rafe's cheek. "I found my handsome prince. Hopefully this little one will someday too. Though I bet Daddy will probably decide the man's not good enough and want to tear apart any guy who tries to get to his baby girl."

"You got that right. Only good things and happy endings for Daddy's girl." Rafe kissed his baby's cheek and got a sock in the nose for it. She was all Lacy with her red hair and pale skin, though it was pink with anger right now as she continued to scream. "I wish she could tell me what's wrong with her. Come on, Daniela, tell Daddy your troubles." Luckily the boys ignored their angry sister and were falling asleep with full tummies.

"Probably a gas bubble. Put her over your shoulder and pat her back, Rafe, while we start loading the car." Sheila grabbed a diaper bag while Lacy picked up an enormous box of disposable diapers and they left the room.

Sheila hadn't gotten near him since they'd arrived. He knew it was because she was waiting for him to sprout horns or something. Rafe didn't blame her for being leery. Lily terrorizing her had sealed the deal as far as in-law relations were concerned. It would be a long time before she trusted him again.

Lacy had tried to calm her mother, even suggesting Sheila visit Ian for a tranquilizer. The fact that her were-cat mother seemed open to the idea had made Lacy roll her eyes. Seems there might be a romantic possibility between the doctor and Mama Cat after all. Who could have predicted that?

Rafe jiggled the baby then held her out from him. "Look at me, Daniela. Seriously, why are you screaming?" She puckered her rosebud mouth, blew a bubble then blinked.

"Oh, shit." Lacy would have his hide for cursing in front of the babies but he couldn't help it. Because there was no mistaking the flash of red he'd seen for just a moment in his little princess's bright blue eyes.

ABOUT THE AUTHOR

The nationally best-selling author of the Real Vampires series, Gerry Bartlett is a native Texan who lives halfway between Houston and Galveston. She freely admits to a shopping addiction which is why she has an antiques business on the historic Strand on Galveston Island. She used to be a gourmet cook but has decided it's more fun to indulge in gourmet eating instead. You can visit Gerry on Facebook, twitter or at her website where she has advice for aspiring writers at http://gerrybartlett.com.

Other Titles by Gerry Bartlett

REAL VAMPIRES HAVE CURVES

REAL VAMPIRES LIVE LARGE

REAL VAMPIRES GET LUCKY

REAL VAMPIRES DON'T DIET

REAL VAMPIRES HATE THEIR THIGHS

REAL VAMPIRES HAVE MORE TO LOVE

REAL VAMPIRES DON'T WEAR SIZE SIX

REAL VAMPIRES HATE SKINNY JEANS

REAL VAMPIRES KNOW HIPS HAPPEN

REAL VAMPIRES KNOW SIZE MATTERS

Novella: REAL VAMPIRES TAKE A BITE OUT OF
CHRISTMAS

REAL VAMPIRES SAY READ MY HIPS

RAFE AND THE REDHEAD

GERRY BARTLETT